THE FORTUNES OF TEXAS

Follow the lives and loves of a complex family with a rich history and deep ties in the Lone Star State

LONE STAR WINDFALL

Secrets once again rock the Texas town of Emerald Ridge! It's tumultuous enough when Archibald Fortune's brother, Clemons, crashes into town. But when a man who's lost his memory arrives with Clemons's name on his lips, the new Fortune siblings are on a mission to discover the truth, no matter the cost...

HER FORTUNE VIP

As he adjusts to his new life as a Fortune, Oakley Fortune's desperate for help at his rodeo business. When Rachel Evers walks through the door, he can't believe his luck—in more ways than one. But Oakley's vindictive father had upended the beautiful single mom's life. Can Oakley convince Rachel to give their arrangement another chance—not only the job, but also what's brewing between them?

Dear Reader,

There's nothing I love more than a great office romance! Navigating those tight-quarter romances, though, can be tricky—which is exactly what Rachel Evers and Oakley Fortune discover.

Once he meets Rachel, Oakley finds he's ready and willing to break the rules. However, he has his work cut out for him, especially when Rachel realizes that Oakley's father is none other than the man who wronged her with a frivolous lawsuit. This determined single mother is not going down without a fight, no matter how fabulous her once-bitten, twice-shy divorced boss is with her nine-month-old daughter, Allie.

I had such fun writing Oakley and Rachel's love story, and I'm delighted to be back with another installment of The Fortunes of Texas, kicking off Oakley and his siblings' journeys to their happily-ever-afters.

Enjoy the romance!

Michele

HER FORTUNE VIP

MICHELE DUNAWAY

THE FORTUNES OF TEXAS

Special thanks and acknowledgment are given to Michele Dunaway for her contribution to The Fortunes of Texas: Lone Star Windfall miniseries.

FSC
www.fsc.org
MIX
Paper | Supporting responsible forestry
FSC® C021394

Recycling programs for this product may not exist in your area.

ISBN-13: 978-1-335-66867-7

Her Fortune VIP

For questions and comments about the quality of this book, please contact us at CustomerService@Harlequin.com.

Harlequin Enterprises ULC
22 Adelaide St. West, 41st Floor
Toronto, Ontario M5H 4E3, Canada
www.Harlequin.com

HarperCollins Publishers
Macken House, 39/40 Mayor Street Upper,
Dublin 1, D01 C9W8, Ireland
www.HarperCollins.com

Printed in Lithuania

1 2 3 4 5 6 7 8 9 10 LIT 28 27 26 25

In first grade, **Michele Dunaway** wanted to be a teacher. In second grade, she wanted to be a writer. By third grade, she decided to be both. Now a bestselling author, Michele strives to create strong heroes and heroines for savvy readers who want contemporary, small-town adventures with characters who discover things about themselves as they travel the road to true love and self-fulfillment. Michele loves to travel, with the places she visits often inspiring her novels. An avid baker, Michele describes herself as a woman who does way too much but never wants to stop, especially when it comes to creating fiction, or baking brownies and chocolate chip cookies. She loves to hear from readers at micheledunaway.com.

Books by Michele Dunaway

Harlequin Special Edition

The Fortunes of Texas: Lone Star Windfall

Her Fortune VIP

Legacy Canyon

A Texas-Sized Fake Out

Love in the Valley

What Happens in the Air
All's Fair in Love and Wine
Love's Secret Ingredient
One Suite Deal
Room for Two More
The Playboy Project

The Fortunes of Texas: Secrets of Fortune's Gold Ranch

Conveniently a Fortune

Visit the Author Profile page at Harlequin.com for more titles.

First and foremost, my readers.
Thank you for letting me be part of your world.

And to my new neighbors (Dave, Darlene, Marty,
Pam and Huey), thank you for the warm welcome.

Chapter One

Rachel Evers needed this job. Not wanted, but *needed.* Not only was she at the end of the figurative rope, but she'd literally drained all of her savings. As her friend and sorority sister Jenny, owner of the Emerald Ridge Employment Agency, had said yesterday, "If you don't land this, I'm not sure what else I can do. I had a glut of jobs when I told you to move here two months ago, and now everything has suddenly dried up."

That pretty much summed up Rachel's life. If bad times came in threes, not finding a job would be the final kiss of death. Not that she had much left to lose. Gone were the days of her cute bungalow in Dallas and her impressive, highly paid office manager job. Gone, too, was the louse who'd skipped town the moment he'd learned she was pregnant, leaving her to be a single mother. Although in hindsight, maybe that was a good thing. She loved her nine-month-old daughter more than anything in the world. Allie was a blessing and a joy, and the thing that kept Rachel going when times looked bleak.

Even after her daughter had been the impetus for that ridiculous lawsuit…

Rachel sighed. The thing about thinking you'd hit rock bottom was you were often wrong and soon discovered there was much further to fall. Maybe bad times actually came in fours or even fives, especially as she'd been "asked to leave" once dealing with said lawsuit had caused her to have too many unexcused absences from work following her maternity leave. At age thirty-two, she'd expected to be applying for better positions and getting promoted, not starting over in the new-to-her town of Emerald Ridge, Texas, after being unemployed since last June. She picked some lint from her skirt. Whoever gave that sound financial advice to have at least three months of expenses saved in cash had been dead-on. She had one month before true desperation struck.

Rachel held out hope that this job was finally the break she needed. She had a good feeling about this opportunity Jenny had found—even if the interview was to have started fifteen minutes ago and the door between the waiting room and the main office remained closed. The desk where an administrative assistant should sit sat empty, the computer monitor black and silent. That would be her spot. Perhaps her boss would even let her put some plants on the windowsill…

Lint dispatched, Rachel smoothed the navy-blue pencil skirt that kept inching up her thighs every time her leg bounced. Catching the anxious quirk, she forced her foot still and shifted on the leather chair. Despite air conditioning working overtime to keep the mid-August morning heat at bay, Rachel tried not to sweat through the matching blazer. As much as she wanted to shed the jacket, she couldn't take it off as it hid the slightly darker baby spit-up stain that lingered on her shoulder, despite her futile dabbing with one of those detergent pens.

Rachel ran a finger under her collar before studying a plain nail kept short in deference to constantly caring for her daughter. Well, that and the fact she couldn't afford regular manicures. It seemed like just yesterday she was giving birth, but time had passed in the blink of an eye, and Allie would be celebrating her first birthday in three months. If Rachel got this job, maybe she could host a real party since she'd once again have steady income, and even more importantly, health insurance. Getting this job would mean she wouldn't have to deliver restaurant and food orders every evening to make ends meet.

Nerves clanging as another minute passed, she checked her phone for the hundredth time in ten minutes. There was nothing from Jenny that the interview had been canceled. Afraid to leave and worried she might look rumpled from the walk over from her apartment, she switched her phone to selfie mode and gave herself one last once-over. Thick straight brows she'd plucked this morning didn't show any stragglers. Her lipstick hadn't smudged, and when she straightened, her blue eyes seemed alert and confident rather than reflecting the constant worry and stress she usually saw.

The door cracked open. "Ms. Evers?"

Rachel rose, glad her stiff legs held her upright, as the most gorgeous man she'd ever seen filled the doorway. Complete with prominent cheekbones and a clean-shaven, defined jawline, he had those ruggedly masculine features that dreams were made of.

Why did he have to look so damn good? Her pulse quickened as bright blue eyes a shade darker than her own met hers. He had that slightly wavy, short dark blond hair a woman's fingers itched to touch. She wanted to run her fingers through the strands and push them away from his forehead. Rachel quivered with awareness. When he reached out his hand to shake hers, she swore her heart pounded and her womb clenched. She somehow ignored the jolt as desire spiked, returning his grip with a firm one of her own, while schooling her expression into neutral. One of her best traits was her professionalism.

"Ms. Evers, I'm Oakley Fros—Fortune. Welcome to Fortune Rodeo Corporation."

"Thank you. It's nice to meet you." Relieved that her voice sounded steady, Rachel resisted the urge to desensitize her tingling fingers by rubbing them with her opposite hand.

"I apologize for the delay. I had a call that ran late. Hopefully you won't hold that against me."

Her *body* wanted to hold his against her. She gave herself a mental scolding and plastered on a reassuring smile. "No worries. Jenny told me you're a busy man." She ignored the way her libido leaped when he gave her an unintentional view of his impressive backside as he led the way into a large but sparsely decorated inner office. Jenny had told Rachel that the previous admin she'd sent to Oakley's office to apply for the job had immediately fallen for him. Rachel could understand why. Oakley was the kind of man Rachel would seek out, if she didn't pride herself on knowing how to check her reactions and remain professional. Then there was the fact she was almost broke…

Oakley paused, and despite being taller than the average woman, she had to glance upward. He topped her easily, even though she was wearing her sensible two-inch pumps. He gave a wide sweep of his arm. "Ignore the mess and lack of decor. I've been way too busy getting buried by paperwork and contracts to decorate."

His polite half smile still had the power to suck the oxygen from the room. He motioned to one of the plush leather armchairs in front of his L-shaped, dark cherrywood desk. "Please take a seat. I'll admit, having to hire a new administrative assistant is new to me. My previous one in Dallas was with me from when I started my company, but she didn't want to relocate to Emerald Ridge, then the one I had when I arrived here..." He shook his head. "Anyway, it didn't work out."

"I'm rather new to town myself," Rachel admitted as she took a seat and watched as Oakley folded himself into his leather office chair.

"Then that makes the pair of us." He lifted a piece of paper.

"It does," she said. As for small talk, it would have to do.

As he read over her résumé, Rachel studied him. Jenny had told her Oakley Fortune was thirty-four and divorced from a cheating ex. "Whatever you do," her friend had warned, "do not ogle him or act unprofessional. I can't have you fired as well for trying to be the next Mrs. Fortune. The first admin I placed with him trapped him in the office kitchen and tried to kiss him, if you can believe it."

Rachel could see why. Oakley's lips were the kind written about in romance novels or seen on the heroes in Netflix rom-coms. She'd reassured Jenny that men were the last thing on her mind. Even though Oakley was the type who might make her change that vow, he wasn't worth losing her job. She'd been through that already, especially after discovering firsthand how her baby daddy had turned into a jerk. Mitch hadn't been her boss or coworker, but he had been a vendor she'd met through her workplace. She wasn't responsible for making her firm's purchasing decisions, so fortunately there wasn't a conflict of interest in their seeing each other. She and Mitch had a great time together, and things seemed to be going well—until she missed her period and two lines appeared on the stick.

Rachel had learned two things from Mitch's desertion. One, she wasn't good at picking men, and two, never date anyone related to your job in even the remotest capacity. Oh, and maybe there was a third thing: find a company that had paid maternity leave. She'd had fun traveling everywhere, meeting Mitch on the road most weekdays or often meeting him for a long weekend, but the end result was that she had almost no PTO saved.

"Tell me about your previous work experience." Oakley's long, firm fingers reached for a pen. "While this role is technically an administrative assistant job, as you can see, it's a two-person office, so essentially you're also the manager. Jenny told me you have experience in that area."

"Yes." As Rachel began to explain her role in her previous firm, she grew more confident, especially as Oakley nodded several times. At the appropriate times he'd add follow-up questions, often jotting down notes.

Once the interview wound down, he asked if she had questions.

"Just the one. I did my research into your firm. As an office, this place seems rather small for the number of people it takes to organize all the rodeos you run across the state."

When he smiled, its warmth and welcome had the impact of a thousand suns. "Actually, that's a good observation. My immediate family recently relocated to Emerald Ridge or is in the process of doing so. My dad is already here, so I came, too. What you see is essentially a two-person satellite office. The main operations remain in Dallas, and you'll act as my liaison between the two offices, while helping set up and run this branch. You can decorate, if you want. I'll give you a generous budget for that."

Meaning she could put her plants on the windowsill. "It could use some life," she said diplomatically.

His laugh was deep, rich and throaty. "Exactly. Eventually, if I choose to stay in Emerald Ridge, I'm envisioning a multiyear transition. I wanted to take some time to settle in and ensure I liked living here before I uprooted my entire company. For now, though, this is home and if I make it permanent, then I'll work on moving everyone else or offering generous severance packages to those employees who don't want to relocate. Like my former Dallas admin who chose the golden parachute and retired."

"Slow and steady sounds like a good plan. It's not as if Dallas is that far of a drive if you need to be there in person when you can't make do with a video call."

"Exactly." He gave a thoughtful nod before studying her for a minute. "I assume Jenny gave you the details? All the fine print as to salary and benefits."

Rachel knew what compensation package Oakley was offering, and it was everything she could have hoped for. Not only did it cover enough for her to afford childcare and her apartment, but after paying off her debt there might be enough left over so she could start saving again, so long as her car didn't die. Plus, after her forty-five-day probationary period, she'd have company-paid health insurance for her and Allie, too. "Yes. Jenny explained the terms and they're acceptable."

"Great." He gave a pleased nod. "In that case, how about you start tomorrow?"

"*Tomorrow?*" She hated the way her voice squeaked. Her start date had come sooner than expected, and now she'd have to find a sitter on short notice.

His golden eyebrow arched in query. "Is that a problem? I've got a busy week filled with meetings, and tomorrow is best for me to get you onboarded. I can have HR reach out this afternoon to set you up with login access, that sort of thing. Jenny told me she already had you fill out all the necessary paperwork."

"She did and starting tomorrow will be fine." Rachel would make it work. Taylor, her elderly neighbor across the hall, had said she'd watch Allie whenever Rachel needed. She was a former early childhood educator and a grandmother, and she'd been a godsend. She'd see if she'd mind doing it until she enrolled Allie in an early childhood center.

"Great. I'll call Jenny so she can get it set up." Oakley stood, indicating the interview was over. He glanced at her fully. "Oh, and one last thing. There's no need to dress up for me. Feel free to be in business casual. Jeans are fine on Friday. If there's an occasion where we need to be more formal, I'll let you know."

"Thank you. I'll make a note of that and dress appropriately." She would *not* make a note of how well his polo and casual pants fit as he rounded the desk. The light from the window behind him created a halo effect, as if the universe emphasized that this job was her salvation. She bit her lower lip as he reached out his hand.

"I'm looking forward to working with you, Rachel. See you tomorrow at eight."

"See you then." She attributed the zing that occurred when he shook her hand to the excitement of landing the most promising job opportunity she'd had in a long while. No more food deliveries…or filling people's grocery orders. She was on her way back to something full-time and permanent.

Her phone rang before she'd reached the apartment she'd rented. The one-bedroom unit was located over Emerald Ridge Yoga & Pilates. Since the studio and the Fortune Rodeo offices were both on Emerald Ridge Boulevard, she'd walked to the interview. The entrance to the building's apartments was down a side street, and Rachel was sweating by the time she climbed the stairs to the second floor. She stepped inside the apartment, stripped off the jacket and shirt clinging to her skin and fanned herself with her hand. Her phone rang again and this time Rachel answered the video call from Jenny. Because she was wearing nothing but her bra and skirt, she pressed the audio-only button.

"Congrats!" her friend said the moment Rachel answered. "I told you that the right thing would come along as long as you were patient. I'm happy for you. I just heard from Oakley, and he mentioned he wants you to start tomorrow."

"That's correct, and thanks—I'm happy for me, too." Unlike Oakley's office, the apartment AC didn't do a good job cooling, so she flipped the switch on a small round fan she'd purchased. Air blessedly began to blow. "I needed this, Jenny."

"I know you did. It's been a rough go these past eighteen months. But you can put it all behind you. Now that you're in Emerald Ridge, you and Allie will get a fresh start. No more Mitch. And the best part? No more Clemons Frost and his frivolous lawsuit."

"That jerk." Rachel had worse words she wanted to say about the pompous man, but thanks to some free-trial yoga classes she'd taken downstairs, she'd been working on using calming techniques to achieve inner peace and Zen. She needed both. The last eighteen months following the discovery of her pregnancy could be described by one word: tumultuous.

Minus the birth of her daughter—Allie would always be a joy and *never* a regret—when it rained it had poured. Not only had Mitch left her high and dry and skipped town so that the lawyer she'd hired couldn't find him to serve him custody paperwork to pay child support, but she'd been in a café when Allie had projectile vomited. The person behind her had been hit, and one Clemons Frost had sued her for one hundred thousand dollars. She didn't even have 2 percent of that in her bank account. Her parents, who were in California, had offered to help with her legal fees, but Rachel had turned them down. They had their own bills following one of the natural disasters that had ravaged the state. While their house had been mostly okay, they'd had minor damage requiring an insurance claim. As for Rachel's siblings, none of them were in a financial position to assist, and they weren't close enough for her to be comfortable asking them anyway.

Thankfully, the judge had tossed out the lawsuit, calling it ridiculous and unwarranted. But the legal costs of defending herself had decimated the majority of her savings. Worse, the unpaid time off she'd had to take following her return from maternity leave had gotten her fired, meaning she was paying out of pocket for both her and the baby's health insurance, something that would soon run out.

Moving to Emerald Ridge marked a new chapter for her. "I'm grateful you told me to come. I'm becoming far more hopeful than I was before."

"I know it's been challenging, and I appreciate you giving me time to get it right," Jenny said. "I'd hire you myself to help me if I wasn't already fully staffed."

Rachel knew she would have. They'd been best friends since they'd pledged the sorority together, and Rachel had stood as a bridesmaid in Jenny's wedding.

"Oh, and while I know I can trust you, I need you to remember that Oakley is a *Fortune*. He's a member of Emerald Ridge's most prominent family. There's the Fortune's Gold Ranch and Spa, there's the cattle operation… I can't even name all of their businesses. That's just this part of Texas. Think fingers in many, many pies, and that's just this branch of the family."

"Wow. Seriously?"

"Yep," Jenny confirmed. "And just because Oakley's offshoot is newer and was discovered because of a DNA test, don't assume they won't close ranks around their own. You need to play it safe around this guy, okay? I met him and he's far too good-looking for his own good. I can see why women would be tempted. If I wasn't happily married…" Jenny's low whistle finished that thought.

"I keep telling you I'm not interested in dating, and anyway, once they find out I have a child, men hit the road. Oakley has nothing to fear from me, not like the last person you placed. The only thing I want from him is my paycheck, good health insurance and a matching 401(k) contribution."

"And I will ensure you get all of that." Jenny sighed. "You know I hated warning you off Oakley. I trust you, which is why I recommended you. You're overqualified, but he's paying well, and you'll do your job without stars in your eyes because you're good at what you do."

"I am," Rachel confirmed as her confidence returned. She had a job. *Finally!* "And Oakley Fortune might be handsome, but I'm a professional. As for my personal life, my main purpose is raising my daughter. Diapers are my priority, not finding Allie a new daddy. That and enrolling her in a great childcare center. I looked into the one out at the Fortune's Gold Ranch, but it's too far and didn't have any openings."

"There's the place just on the edge of town," her bestie said. "It's not too far."

"Already on it. I sent them an email and I've got an appointment lined up. I'm hoping that the fee is reasonable and there's space available. I can't keep asking Taylor to watch Allie."

"I've helped the owner find employees before. Let me make a phone call and see if I can pull some strings on your behalf. And, as for you and me, we need to celebrate. Let's do dinner later this week. Lee is golfing with his dad on Friday and his mom will take the kids. What about then? On me, of course, since I'm getting a hefty commission. I'll find someplace where we can bring Allie. Besides, I'll want to hear about how your first week went."

"That sounds perfect. Friday it is."

Rachel ended the call and leaned against the couch. She wasn't a huge believer in astrology, but in a bout of curiosity, a few days ago she'd clicked one of those stories that had come through her news feed. The next sixty days were supposedly going to bring good things to those of her astrological sign. Until now, the horoscope had been wishful thinking for a girl at her wit's end. She couldn't take any more setbacks or disappointments.

Sighing, she rose, put on a shirt and went to retrieve Allie. Her neighbor had an appointment, so the handoff was quick. Rachel would have to chat with her later about babysitting.

"Guess what," Rachel cooed to Allie as they entered their apartment. "Mommy got a new job."

The nine-month-old's blue eyes blinked, and she offered Rachel her pacifier. Smiling down at her daughter, Rachel took the Binky and popped it back into Allie's mouth. "Let's get some lunch, shall we?" She set her baby girl in the high chair and gave her a few cut-up strawberries. Allie took one in her fist and shoved it in her mouth before laughing. Rachel inhaled deeply as the instructor had taught her. Everything was going to be okay.

She'd run an office of sixty people before, and she could easily handle an office consisting of just one other person. Even if Oakley made her heart race, he was safe. He'd hired someone once burned, twice shy, and three times more determined never to make the same mistakes again.

Chapter Two

About a week after Rachel had started as his admin, Oakley Fortune considered himself a happy camper. Not that he'd been a Boy Scout when younger or actually gone camping, except for that one time with his best friend's family, and they'd roughed it in a lodge. But he was truly satisfied and content with his new administrative assistant. Rachel was a gem. She was thorough and knowledgeable and could anticipate his needs, even bringing him coffee before he needed a cup. While it wasn't in her job description to serve him coffee, she'd said that since she was making a fresh pot anyway, it wasn't that big of a deal. He'd taken her at her word, especially as her actions had made it clear she wasn't using it as an excuse to talk with him like the previous Emerald Ridge admin.

He'd learned that Rachel said what she needed to say and then returned to her desk, their conversations having revolved around business and nothing more. She was curious about how to best manage his office and his schedule, and within a day she'd taken over. Clark Adams, Oakley's executive VP and best friend, had remarked how professional Rachel had been during her interactions with those in the Dallas office. In a literal sense, she was a godsend. Unlike her immediate predecessor, Rachel didn't flirt or ask personal questions. He didn't either, although he found himself curious. Minus what Jenny at the employment agency had told him, he didn't have much intel on his admin. He knew Rachel had a baby and two parents, but only because she'd set photos of each on her desk. There was no photo of a boyfriend, but Rachel had mentioned Taylor was watching Allie, so he assumed that was his admin's partner. She had also brought in two houseplants that added a pop of green to the windowsill. When he'd asked about her daughter's name, her face had brightened, and he'd liked her smile.

Oakley stepped out into the exterior office. "I'm off to meet my father for lunch. I'll be back later on today. If anyone calls, please take a message."

"Sounds good. Mail should be here soon. I'll open it and put it on your desk." She didn't even glance up from the email she was typing, which slightly disappointed him. She had beautiful blue eyes and he enjoyed gazing into them and trying to guess what she was thinking. She'd taken the business casual to heart, wearing dress pants and short-sleeved sweaters to the office. Her long dark hair was normally in a ponytail or a knot of some sort, the latter revealing a long, smooth neck.

"Thank you. Appreciate it." He also liked how she sorted his mail, making it easy for him to get through the dreaded daily chore. "Unless the world is ending, no need to contact me until I get back."

"See you then." Without breaking her concentration from the work on her computer, she gave him an offhand wave.

Oakley left the office and headed out of the building. At the corner, he crossed the boulevard and strolled through the city park until he reached the entrance to the river promenade, a concrete waterfront path that followed the curve of the Emerald Ridge River. Built ten years prior, the promenade was akin to Austin's hiking and biking trail around Lady Bird Lake or the San Antonio River Walk, but without the size or scale of either. It did, however, give an excellent view of the river below.

As he strode along at a rapid pace, Oakley passed by couples sitting on the benches and people reading the historic markers telling the town's story. The walkway meandered under heritage trees that provided shade. A few paths led to dedicated fishing spots often used by anglers or those seeking selfies. He stepped aside as a mother pushing a stroller jogged by him. Two people cruising at top speed in motorized wheelchairs followed her. He passed the adjoining sidewalk that led to the Victorian-style gazebo and took the next set of stairs. These led to the Riverside Café, which featured farm-to-table dining and excellent river views from both the inside tables and those on the deck.

He found his father inside by the windows, in a prime spot.

"There you are," Clemons Fortune grumbled as Oakley sat across from him. "Was about to give up on you."

"I said I'd be here at noon and I am." Oakley shifted and reached for the water glass.

"Harrumph." Clemons turned to watch someone walk past. Today he wore his favorite white linen suit, the one that Oakley's younger sister had said made their dad look "dapper." Clemons's custom Stetson, which sat atop a head of unruly silver hair, completed the look. In contrast, Oakley was in khakis and a polo, something that elicited another deep disapproving frown. "Son, you can buy fancier clothes. We're Fortunes now. Need to look and dress the part."

"Uh-huh," Oakley murmured noncommittally. As the oldest male sibling, he'd been managing his father for the better part of his life. Best to let the old man say his peace so they could move on to better topics.

"We wouldn't be here had I not taken the DNA test," Clemons continued.

"No, we would not," Oakley agreed before he ordered a lemonade from the server who brought him a menu. Because their family was tight, and so they could stay close to their widowed dad, he and his siblings had made a conscious decision to follow him to Emerald Ridge. Hence Oakley's satellite office and his need for a new admin.

"Who would have thought I had a long-lost older half brother?" Clemons mused.

"Not me," Oakley said as he did each time.

"Strange thing," his dad added.

"Uh-huh." Oakley knew the entire story. His father had been adopted as a baby by a rich Dallas family, and he'd had a privileged upbringing. However, his adoptive parents believed in hard work. Clemons hadn't received a financial handout and wouldn't until they passed, if then.

As for his birth family, DNA had revealed a long-lost older brother, Archibald, who'd struck it rich in the airline industry as a young adult after getting a small loan from Kate Fortune, a distant relation who'd recently turned one hundred. Clemons had crashed her big birthday soiree when he'd first arrived in Emerald Ridge. Oakley hoped his dad hadn't asked her for a handout, too.

"So, I was looking into some business opportunities," Clemons began.

This made Oakley pay better attention. Even before

the death of his wife, Randa, mother to Oakley and his siblings, their father had often started a series of dopey businesses, all of which had failed. He'd also had a few justifiable lawsuits, but after her death, Clemons had kept going with even more frivolous suits, realizing he could line his coffers by being sue-happy. As his dad talked, Oakley didn't believe his newest harebrained scheme would merit him actually following through. No need to worry on that account—yet.

"Took the liberty of ordering a meal for you since you were so late," his dad said as the server returned with Oakley's lemonade. "Got you a grilled chicken sandwich."

"I was not even three minutes late," he protested. Oakley resisted clenching his fists in frustration and instead placed them flat on the table.

His father's steely blue gaze pinned him with the full weight of his fatherly disapproval. "If you're not five minutes early, you're late."

"Not in Emerald Ridge." Time moved slower here than it did in Dallas, which was something Oakley had discovered and already enjoyed. People in Dallas had been friendly with full-on Texas hospitality, whereas folks in Emerald Ridge were ten times as warm—a feat Oakley would have thought impossible had he not seen and experienced it firsthand. Partly because he and his siblings had wanted to get to know their long-lost family and partly to keep watch on their dad, they'd joined Clemons in changing their surname from Frost to Fortune when following him to Emerald Ridge.

Their server returned, carrying two plates. Each contained fries, a small house salad and a loaded chicken sandwich. Clemons lifted the artisanal bun and scowled.

"Look at the size of this chicken breast. There's nothing there. What am I paying these ridiculous prices for?"

"Dad," Oakley warned. He prayed no one had overheard. Already his father had thrown a fit in The Style Lounge over his "imperfect" haircut and refused to pay. He'd also sent back three very expensive bottles of Leonetti Vineyards wine the other night at Captain's, the town's swankiest restaurant. He'd said they tasted "off." While not a sommelier, Oakley knew enough about wine to know the bottles had been fine, perfectly palatable and eminently drinkable. "Dad, relax. It's organic, free-range chicken. It's not bred to have breasts the size of your hand."

Clemons rolled his eyes and took a bite. "See," Oakley said after he finished his own morsel. "It's delicious."

Being stubborn, Clemons didn't acknowledge that assertion. Instead he said, "So, business stuff aside, I thought you'd like to know I found a new attorney, one local to Emerald Ridge."

"Dad, no." Oakley's condemnation was quick. His father was always suing someone, and it had gotten tiresome, not to mention embarrassing.

"No, what?" Clemons replied. He dangled a thick-cut fry from his fingertips as if it, too, wouldn't suit. "I need a lawyer."

"No, you don't. We moved here for a fresh start. I've got my offices in the same building as some of the other Fortunes. You need to rein it in. You have more than enough money."

Clemons snorted at that statement. "Our branch of the Fortunes is *not* rich."

It was true that this side of the Fortune family was much less affluent, with the exception of Clemons and his late half brother Archibald. But that didn't matter.

Their reputation did. Oakley's own company was now the *Fortune* Rodeo Corporation. They had to live up to the moniker.

"You have plenty of money. You are well-off, and you promised all us kids you'd turn over a new leaf in Mom's honor." Oakley watched as Clemons pushed his plate toward the center of the table, his dissatisfaction evident. "Dad, come on. There is nothing wrong with the food. It's delicious. Eat."

That earned him another snort, and Oakley wondered if the five-year mark of his mother's death was causing his father to have a resurgence of grief and loneliness. Could that be the reason he was acting out? His dad hadn't dated at all since his wife passed.

"Dad, you're better than this. You know Mom would not be happy to hear you've been suing everyone. It's been almost five years, and you know she'd want you to be happy. Maybe it's time to move on. Get back on the horse so to speak. Maybe go on a date or two."

That had his father bolting to his feet. He hovered over the table. "How dare you speak of your mother like you know what she'd want for me! She was a saint. You have some gall suggesting these things, as if I'm not a grown man who knows the difference between right and wrong or when it's the time to date. Bad enough you kids are all coming here to keep tabs on me as if I'm some geriatric invalid." He hovered over the table, glowering down at him. "Boy, you're not only trying to poison everyone against me with these accusations, but you're bordering on disrespect. You need to watch yourself. I didn't raise you to be like this."

His father had directed his tirades at Oakley before,

but this one stung. "I didn't say to forget Mom. Did you hear me say those words?" Oakley argued.

Clemons's answer was to walk out of the restaurant. *Stormed* might be a more apt description since people began looking at his father. Oakley shook his head in disbelief. Having learned to always carry a wad of cash for these exact situations, he peeled off some bills, tossed them on the table and followed.

"Dad!" he shouted, but his sixty-eight-year-old father kept going. As his dad was tall and in good shape, Oakley increased his pace to keep up. He finally caught him along the promenade.

"Dad, stop it," Oakley commanded. He didn't have kids, and perhaps he was being somewhat disrespectful to think this way, but this felt akin to being a parent dealing with a wayward child. You loved them, but at the same time were also frustrated beyond belief. "*Dad! Stop!*"

His father stopped. But it wasn't because he was waiting for Oakley. Instead, he pointed through some trees to a lump along the edge of the river. "What the heck is that?" Clemons asked.

A man with a huge gash on his head lay at the bottom of the steep hill, pressed up against some trees. Oakley gasped. His shock lasted a split second, and then he was on the move. "We have to help him."

He started down the hill toward the bank, trying to keep his balance on the uneven slope. When they reached the man, Clemons leaned over him. "Is he alive?" Oakley asked.

"Yes. Thank goodness he's breathing." Clemons gestured toward where the man's chest rose and fell. "But it seems he's hurt bad. Look at that wound."

Oakley already had his phone out. He dialed 9-1-1 and

reported the incident. "What does he look like?" the dispatcher asked after he gave her their location.

"He appears to be late thirties. Blue eyes. Brown hair. Tall and muscular. Wearing jeans, a Western-style flannel shirt and sneakers."

"Okay, can you stay on the line?" the operator asked.

"No, I need to help him, and yes, I know not to move him," Oakley told her. Since first responders were on the way, he hung up. The other reason he wanted off the call was because his father was nosily searching the man's pockets. "Dad! What the hell are you doing? Stop that. Leave that to the police!"

In true form, his father ignored him. "Need to know who this guy is. Doesn't have a wallet on him. What's this?"

From the pocket of the man's shirt, Clemons withdrew two things. "Look at these." He held them out for Oakley to see. The first was a photo of a smiling baby that looked strangely familiar. But then, Oakley figured, didn't all babies sort of look the same, especially at that age? Turning the photo over revealed there was nothing written on the back, not even a printed lab development coding or the date. The second item was an envelope with one sheet of paper inside. "Looks like a letter," Clemons said. He unfolded it and read, "*I think of you often and hope you forgive me.*" He looked at Oakley and shrugged. "What's that mean?"

"No idea. Put them back!"

The sound of sirens reached them, and at the top of the hill people were starting to gather and peer through the trees toward the riverbank. Clemons quickly restored the items to where he found them. The police arrived along with the paramedics. A flurry of activity commenced as the EMTs triaged the man before loading him onto a gurney. This allowed Oakley to study the man, whose face was pale and still and covered in blood.

"Have you seen him before?" one of the officers asked.

"No, I haven't," Oakley told her. "He looks a little bit like Henry Cavill. But it's not."

"Wouldn't that have been something?" The officer gave a wistful half smile and faced Clemons. "And you? Have you seen the guy around town in the past few weeks?"

Clemons's offhand shrug seemed forced. "No. Never. No clue who he is."

"Seems like we have ourselves a John Doe until he wakes up." The officer recorded their names and contact information in her notebook. The paramedics began pushing the gurney up the hill, and once at the road, loaded the man into the ambulance, and then took off. Some of the police officers followed the ambulance while others processed the scene.

"Wow. Wild, right? Certainly not what I was expecting to see today," Oakley remarked as he and his dad climbed the hill. When they reached the path, Clemons checked the hem of his suit and grimaced at the grass stains near the heel. "Look at my clothes. This better come out or the dry cleaners and I will be having words."

"I'm sure they'll make it good as new. And I wonder what could have happened? Do you think that man was robbed?"

He had no wallet. If the trees hadn't been there, would he have ended up in the river? Had someone pushed him off the promenade, or had he simply slipped and fallen? Down below the police officers bent over something. Oakley couldn't hear what was being said, but one of them took notes.

"I hope he's okay," Oakley said.

"Should be," Clemons mused. "Guy had to have been mugged. Won't be surprised if that's what the cops say. This town isn't so picture-postcard perfect as it pretends to be. You may tell me to calm down, but you're wrong. I have a right to complain. It's no better here than anywhere else. That guy is proof that Emerald Ridge isn't all it's cracked up to be."

Oakley sighed. "Dad," he began.

Clemons jabbed a finger in the air. "Don't 'Dad' me. I'm no pushover. Just because I'm new here doesn't mean I'm gonna let people in this town take advantage of me. I've made my money fair and square."

Some would say that Clemons had made his money by abusing the tort system, but even Oakley had to admit that his dad had been justified in some of his causes. The problem was Clemons had far too many causes. He was like Giles Corey in *The Crucible*, Oakley's favorite play—much put-upon and ready to get justice when he thought he was right, which most times he wasn't. Then again, Giles Corey was also deeply courageous and stood strong on his convictions. He was definitely a paradox, just like Oakley's father.

Shoving a hand through his hair, he cut his father off before he delved into another litany. "I'll check in with the officers later and see if I can find out anything about him. I'll keep you posted."

"Do. I'm going to go home and feed Mewington. Darn cat only likes the fancy wet food, that expensive stuff in the small can. He eats better than me."

His dad leveled that complaint with affection, for Mewington was Clemons's beloved, two-year-old Maine coon cat. Upon learning that their father had had a Maine coon when he was younger, Oakley and his siblings had found the purebred cat at a local shelter and taken their dad to an adoption event. It had been love at first sight for everyone.

Oakley's baby sister, Cheyenne, had even gotten Mewington a diamond-studded pink collar, which Oakley found funny as the cat was a neutered male. But as Cheyenne had said, fixed cats were now considered an *it*, and that meant they could wear whatever they wanted, and besides, Clemons had liked the way the pink color had popped against Mewington's fluffy brown fur. The Maine coon was spoiled rotten. Not only did Clemons brush him every day, but he'd also built Mewington a catio in the river-view house he'd rented for the year. That way the kitty could be safely outside and get fresh air and touch grass while being contained.

"Give Mews a scratch for me. I'll text you later." Near the parking lot, Oakley separated from his father and walked back through the park toward Emerald Ridge Boulevard. He wondered what Rachel would think about the man on the riverbank. He also wondered if she was hungry. Because of his father's abrupt exit from the table, Oakley hadn't gotten a chance to eat his chicken sandwich and fries, and his stomach grumbled its displeasure. He entered the lobby and pressed the elevator Up button. Because he had a conference call in ten minutes, he'd ask Rachel to order him something, and he'd treat her out of the office budget if she wanted something for herself. That was legal, and the least he could do since he was asking her to place the order.

He stepped off the elevator, walked down the hall, then reached for the door handle to his office and gave a pull. His arm jerked as he found the place locked. That was strange. He retrieved his key and unlocked the door. The reception area looked as it always had. A row of leather chairs along one wall. Along another, a leather love seat with a coffee table. There was the water cooler and the side table with a few rodeo magazines. Sun streamed through the window and a beam fell on his administrative assistant's desk.

A desk that was empty. Her computer was dark-screened and silent—turned off and not simply asleep. He checked his phone. Odd. Rachel hadn't texted him. He logged into an app on his phone and opened his email. Nothing there either. Had she stepped out and forgotten to tell him? Things had definitely taken a strange turn. First, they'd found the man on the riverbank and now he was missing his admin.

He entered his personal office, sat down behind his desk and found his mail stacked neatly, exactly as it should be. Letters he needed to deal with immediately were in one pile. Bills in another and junk mail in a third. To the right of those, a package from his sister was resting on top of the box she'd shipped it in. He lifted the framed photo, the last one taken before their mother had gotten sick. Underneath the frame he found a sticky note in Rachel's handwriting. *I'm sorry. I can't do this. I'm quitting effective immediately. Thanks, but no thanks. Sorry.*

Her double "sorry" gutted him. What had made her decide to quit? He stared at the photo of everyone smiling. *No. Please don't let it be.*

With a sick feeling churning in his gut, he roused his computer and did a quick internet search using two names: Rachel Evers and Clemons Frost. The results loaded immediately, most of them news articles with headlines reading something like "Man sues woman and her baby for mental distress after baby vomits on his back and shoulder."

Most of the comments accompanying the article were filled with vitriol, calling his father all sorts of names. Multiple witnesses said Rachel had attempted to pay Clemons's dry-cleaning bill. She'd apologized to him and to everyone in the shop. But his father had still sued her for one hundred thousand dollars. Oakley dropped his head in his hands as shame filled him. Then he found himself angry on her behalf. He'd hired her through an employment agency. She must have assumed he'd always been a Fortune since that was his last name, but once she'd opened his mail and seen the family photo, she realized he was also Oakley Frost, and that his father, Clemons Frost, was the litigant.

Oakley scowled. His dad had just cost him one of the best administrative assistants he'd ever had, and given what Oakley had just discovered, he couldn't blame her for leaving. Irritation coursed through him as he picked up his phone and dialed. When his father answered, Oakley forced himself to unclench his jaw.

"Did you find out anything?" his father asked.

"No," he clipped out. "Instead, I was just reading about your lawsuit where you sued a woman because her baby accidentally threw up on you. What were you *thinking*?" And how had he missed that lawsuit? Oakley knew about the too-hot coffee that had scalded his dad, the faulty siding that had buckled and warped and caused water damage, and the store that hadn't wiped up spilled water, causing his dad to slip and sprain his ankle. Yet somehow, this ridiculous litigation involving his admin had slipped completely under his radar.

"I was thinking her baby puked on my nice new linen

suit. Even after dry cleaning, it wasn't the same. And it was *vomit.* It caused emotional distress," Clemons said.

Once again, Oakley wanted to put his head in his hands, this time to scream in frustration. But he refrained. The truth was plain to see—at times his dad was a menace, and like a leopard, he couldn't change his spots.

Who sued a woman whose baby accidentally vomited? His father did. The suit had dry-cleaned just fine, but his father had refused to wear it again and had donated the "offensive item." If his dad didn't change his ways, so much for a fresh start. Apparently, Clemons's actions had already followed them here.

"Dad, you have to stop this. Emerald Ridge is not Dallas. It's a small town. You're going to get a terrible reputation and ruin everything. You've already insulted the Leonetti family."

Oakley held out his phone just as his father let loose in his ear. When he quieted, Oakley said simply, "You just cost me the best admin I've had in forever, and I can't let this stand."

"How did I do that?"

As his father wound up his justifications again, the video call Oakley was expecting from his sister rang, and Oakley hung up on his dad. He didn't have the patience to listen any longer. His sister was already online when he joined.

"Sorry, I'm a bit early," Cheyenne, the youngest sibling, said. "Did you hear about the man they found in the park? I was in the ER when it happened."

"Actually, Dad and I were the ones to find him." He told her what he'd seen until the rest of the siblings came online.

"And I thought *I* was early," his sister Maisey quipped as she joined them.

Jagger, Evanston and Avery came online next. The siblings were close, and they chatted virtually at least once a week to touch base. Normally, the conversation revolved around their father, and this time was no different.

"I'm worried Dad's reverting back to his 'let's sue everyone' behavior," Oakley grumbled.

"Please, no," Maisey said. "None of us needs that. This was to be a clean slate for him."

"Well, apparently he lost the memo." Oakley sighed. "We're almost to the anniversary of losing Mom. Could that be why he's acting out more than usual? You should have seen how furious he got when I suggested maybe it was time to move on."

His siblings made sympathetic noises. "I just want him happy," he added. "It was rough, losing her, but he needs to heal."

Their mother had been sick for a while, in and out of hospitals, but after the brain tumor manifested, she'd been gone in days.

"We all do," Jagger said. He hadn't made it back to their mom's bedside in time, and Oakley knew his brother still blamed himself. "And we want him to find happiness again."

"Exactly," he agreed. "We can't let Dad blow this chance for a do-over. We have to do something to help him get through this. He's a Fortune now—we all are—and we can't destroy our family's reputation in this town. Our new relations will never forgive us…and I'd prefer they not shun us before we get fully settled."

As the siblings began to discuss ideas, Oakley picked up the sticky note Rachel had left. He turned it over and over in his fingertips. Resolve set in. He had to admit he was like his father in one aspect. When wronged, he took action.

He wasn't going to let this injustice stand.

Chapter Three

Rachel's hands shook as she changed Allie's diaper. As her baby happily kicked her legs and chortled, she inhaled a deep breath. Rachel counted to four slowly before letting it out over a count of eight. Her daughter didn't need to know how livid her mom was at this cruel twist of fate. She tickled Allie's bare feet, making her laugh more. Then she scooped her baby girl into her arms and carried her from the bedroom back into the living room, where she set her in the playpen.

"You okay?" Jenny asked. She'd rushed over as soon as Rachel had called and given her the news. "I mean, I know the answer to that question… But you still look shaken."

Rachel bit back the tears threatening to fall. "I'll be okay. Seriously. I've been through worse, right? I really liked this job." She also needed the money, and the health insurance. Also, walking out meant no reference. But there was no way she could stay.

"I know you did, and I promise I will find you another one." Jenny patted the couch cushion, and Rachel sat. "*You* are my priority. I'm glad you called me."

"Me too. Thank you." Tears raced down Rachel's cheeks.

"Oh, honey, where else would I be?"

"Work?" Even to her own ears, Rachel's joke came

across half-hearted and sad. She swiped her eyes with her sleeve.

"Being the boss has to have some perks. One is being able to leave in an emergency," Jenny said. "I got you into this, and I'll help you get out. I have faith this will be okay."

"But I could have ruined things for your business."

"You didn't, and I'll handle it if necessary. Friends first, *always*."

Rachel reached for her wineglass. Upon hearing what had happened, Jenny had left work early and brought over takeout and a bottle of Rachel's favorite Merlot. She was a loyal friend who'd declared it was five o'clock somewhere. "I'll let the rest of tonight be my pity party, and then tomorrow I'll figure things out. Hit the ground running." Rachel's attempt at projecting confidence and bravado rang flat.

"That sounds like a good plan." Jenny sipped her own wine. "I still can't believe that Clemons Frost and Clemons Fortune are the same person. The Fortunes must be beside themselves to have to claim that man because of his DNA." She huffed out a breath. "Did you hear about how he sent back three bottles of Leonetti wine? Leo Leonetti is married to Poppy Fortune. Talk about crass! Not to mention failing to read the room. I heard the wine was fine—as if Leo would let a bad vintage leave his vineyard."

"He's a horrible, horrible man. He made my life a living hell. I moved to Emerald Ridge to escape him. How's that for irony?" Rachel took another gulp of wine. "I can't believe this happened. Or that my excellent boss is his son. Who or what did I cross to deserve this?"

"There's no way either of us could have known," Jenny soothed.

"Clemons Frost—I mean Fortune," Rachel spit out the

name, "cost me everything. My job. My house. Once I saw that photo and after I did an internet search, I had to quit. How can I trust that Oakley is not like his father? Maybe he'd hired me because he wanted to toy with me?" She set the empty glass on the table and, glancing over at Allie, was relieved to see her daughter happily playing with blocks. "I'm sorry if this made things awkward for you."

"You keep saying that, so believe me when I say it's okay. I might lose Oakley Fortune's business, but I won't lose anyone else's. My clients know me. You did the right thing, quitting like that." She reached and gave Rachel's knee a little squeeze. "You are my friend. That's not changing. I support you fully."

"Thank you. That means a lot. When I saw that photo…" Her voice choked. "Clemons ruins everything. Why did he have to ruin *this*? I mean, look at this place. Haven't I suffered enough? The guy has grown kids. You're telling me they never once threw up?"

Instead of looking at the chic shabbiness of the furnishings Rachel had cobbled together, Jenny gathered Rachel into an enormous hug. "It's going to be okay. Trust me. You will get through this. This, too, shall pass."

"I hope so." Drawing back, Rachel watched as Allie pulled herself up and stood holding on to the side of the playpen before plopping back down. Rachel's mom had told her that she'd walked early, and it appeared as if her baby girl would do the same. "It would be so different if I didn't have to think about Allie. I could go anywhere and do anything…but I have to put my daughter first. We're a team. She's what matters."

"You're a great mom." Jenny's phone beeped, and she checked the message. "Speaking of being a mom, my husband just sent me a message. It's clearly something he can't handle, so I have to go home." She sighed. "He's lucky I love him."

"I know you wish he'd step up a bit more in the fatherhood department, but we both know he's a keeper. And I appreciate the late lunch and you attempting to cheer me up." She walked Jenny to the front door and accepted another hug. "Tell Lee I said hi."

"I will and I'll call you tomorrow." Jenny stepped into the hall and Rachel closed the door behind her. Turning back to check on Allie, she saw her daughter bending and straightening her legs as she clung to the side of the playpen. "That's right, Allie. Work those legs! Speaking of which, I should do some yoga..."

Not that the apartment had much room to move around. While it had one bedroom, the place was a mere four hundred square feet, and much of it was crammed with the things she hadn't been able to part with when she'd moved from Dallas. Most of her possessions remained in the moving boxes as she had no idea where to put anything, and she didn't have the room anyway. She'd hoped to get a good job so she could move into something bigger, where Allie didn't have to have a crib in the same room as her mom. She'd have to put that dream on hold. Having a brief window of time, she turned on her laptop and scoured the online job boards. The results were depressing. As if sensing her mother's worry, Allie began to cry.

Rachel rose and handed her daughter her pacifier, but that didn't work. Nor did picking her up. Instead, Allie's face reddened, and she cried harder. A diaper check revealed that wasn't the problem.

"Okay, let me go make you something." She put her daughter in the high chair and gave her some Cheerios. Allie ate some of the oat circles while Rachel began to clean a prep area by shoving the empty carryout containers into the trash can. Like diapers, trash bags were expensive and a big part of her budget. As one of the boxes' sharp corners caught the bag, the plastic tore. *Figured.* She'd take the trash down later to the dumpster located in the alley.

In the high chair, Allie started crying again. "I'm coming, sweetie," Rachel said, scrambling to measure the formula.

Mid-scoop, a knock sounded on her front door. Either Jenny had forgotten something, which was unlikely as she'd been gone for over an hour, or it was Taylor, her retired neighbor from across the hall. In a hurry, Rachel opened the door without looking through the peephole. She recoiled as she found Oakley Fortune standing there.

Her first reaction was to close the door, but his hand stopped her. He didn't push back, though, or try to enter. "Please talk to me." He held up a bag. "I brought dinner."

In the tiny dining area, Allie screamed louder. Rachel glanced over her shoulder. "That's kind but as you can hear, I've got to go. Besides, I've eaten. Jenny brought us burgers and fries for a late lunch."

"Then you can eat your share tomorrow. It's chicken spiedini from Cucina. It should reheat." Oakley stretched the bag forward, and she smelled hints of garlic.

Cucina was the Italian restaurant located in the Emerald Ridge Hotel. The ambience was romantic and the bill expensive. For those reasons alone, she'd had no reason to go there, but she had heard the food was delicious. She opened the door wider and reached for the bag. "Okay, you can come in. I suppose I should explain, and I need to get my daughter."

Allie, as if sensing a visitor, chose to scream even louder.

"If it's because of what I read on the internet after I got your note, no explanation is needed. No one should have put you through that." Oakley stepped into the apartment, which made the place shrink. Rachel was also immediately aware of how shabby it must look. Even the leather chairs in the waiting room of his office were of better quality than the two metal chairs located at the minuscule kitchen table. From the cutout in the wall between the kitchen and dining area, Rachel watched as Oakley stopped about five feet from Allie's high chair.

"Hey there," Oakley said. "Aren't you a pretty little thing."

For a brief second, Allie stopped crying. Then she started again. "Really?" Oakley teased Allie. "Tell me more. Let me hear all about it…"

As Allie's cry died in her throat, Rachel quickly shoved the oversize white take-out bag into the refrigerator, checked that the sippy cup full of formula was the right temperature and headed toward them. Finally quiet, Allie stared at Oakley with huge, interested blue eyes and mouth as wide as Palo Duro Canyon. She couldn't blame her daughter. Oakley *was* impressive.

"She needs to eat." But when Rachel handed Allie the cup, her daughter threw it. Then, when Rachel returned the cup to the tray, she began to cry again and hold up her arms. Rachel lifted her from the high chair, but she couldn't calm her. Allie leaned and dove toward Oakley.

"May I?" he asked, putting his arms out.

"Sure." Rachel wasn't certain why she passed over Allie to a man whose father had sued her, but for some unknown reason—maybe it was simply that her daughter had the lungs of an opera singer and today Rachel couldn't endure any more stress—she let Oakley hold Allie.

Allie immediately stopped crying. Her hands went to

Oakley's chin, which she patted. He took the cup from the tray and gave it to Allie. "Time to drink that," he told the child. To Rachel's surprise, she did.

"You have a way with her," she said, amazed. "Allie's normally not like this with strangers, but she likes you."

"I love babies. Thought I'd have one or two of my own by now." He glanced at Rachel. "Did you put the food away?"

"I did. It's in the fridge."

"Do you mind if I eat my portion? Been dealing with a few things and haven't had anything since lunch, which I didn't get to eat but three bites of. Long story, which we can also blame on my father."

"Uh, sure. Sorry." Didn't she feel foolish? She retrieved the bag of food as her daughter went willingly into her high chair and Oakley secured her. Rachel handed him the bag, and he spread out the contents on the small table. He held out a see-through plastic container. "Sure you don't want something more than a burger?"

It had been a few hours, and Rachel had skipped lunch. She'd also picked at the food Jenny had brought. "I'll eat a little." After pouring two glasses of water, she joined him at the small table and opened her container. Allie sat between them on one side of the table. Rachel grabbed one of the plastic forks and stuck it into the chicken, taking a bite and finding it every bit as delicious as the reviews said. Same for the thick and creamy white pasta served as the side.

"I want to apologize," Oakley began. "First, for my father, because what he did was *inexcusable*. He owes you one, too, and someday I'll ensure you get it. Second, I'm apologizing that you had to find out he and I are related by opening the mail. We came to Emerald Ridge for a fresh start, which was one reason for the name change. Another reason we moved was because it's been almost five years since we lost our mom. My siblings and I thought that getting to know our biological family could be a good thing for him."

"I'm sorry for your loss." She didn't see her parents often, but they video-called at least once a week.

"Thanks. My dad took it hard, and his behavior sort of went off the rails. He's never made a genuine success of any of his business endeavors, and maybe winning his court litigations filled the void left by my mom's death. He was justified some of the time, but in your situation, he wasn't. I'm glad the case was thrown out."

Rachel appreciated his apology but couldn't forgive. Not that easily. "Yes, but not without ruining me financially. That's why I moved to Emerald Ridge. To start over, too." She gestured wildly around the room. "This is not what my life was like. I was successful. I had a house. Do you know how much good defense lawyers cost? Far more than buying your father a brand-new suit. Why did he even think I had one hundred thousand dollars? Who wears a white suit in public anyway? White fabric is a dirt magnet."

As if proving the point, Allie dribbled some formula on her "*I love Mommy*" bib.

"The white linen suit is his trademark." About to say something else, Oakley shook his head as if to clear it. "Which doesn't matter. Nothing I say can make up for the pain he put you through."

"You think?" Fueled by pent-up anger, Rachel nearly lost it. "He doesn't consider anyone else but himself. Now he's moved somewhere new and is already up to his old tricks. Doesn't he know that Leo Leonetti is married to

Poppy Fortune? Who belittles their own family? That's why I had to quit. I can't trust that more bad things won't happen. And I can't be guilty by association, either. I will not be party to Clemons's lack of civility."

Oakley exhaled. "Believe me, I can understand that and won't hold it against you. But you can trust me."

"That's the trouble—I can't. I've been burned too many times to trust anyone that freely again. I liked working for you…but I can't help worrying that the apple doesn't fall far from the tree."

He set his fork down. "I'm on your side, Rachel. My siblings and I had a conference call this afternoon. While we didn't talk about you, my siblings and I did discuss how our dad needs to tone down his behavior. That he can't keep suing people. It reflects poorly on us, as evidenced by your leaving. And you've become important to me, to my business. Even though it's been a week, I never thought I'd find an admin like the one who retired, and yet there you were. I want you back."

The declaration sent a shiver through her, but she couldn't trust the words.

"You're just saying that because you feel sorry for me," Rachel said. "You waltz in here with food I never could afford because your father has embarrassed you again. Jenny will find someone else to replace me in your Emerald Ridge office. Third time's the charm and all that."

"I don't want someone else—I want *you*." His assertion punctuated each word. Oakley was a man who knew what he wanted, which, right now, was her.

"What will it take? A pay raise? Done. Benefits immediately? Done. Childcare allowance? Done. You name it, Rachel. If it's in my power, I'll make it happen."

She stared at him with the same wide eyes as Allie

had had earlier. "You don't mean that. Stop insulting my pride… I can't be bought."

"I'm dead serious. I'm not playing you, and I'm not trying to buy you. I want to *rehire* you. I can't make up for what my father did, but I can make your employment the best it can be. You need a job, and I need an administrative assistant who gets me. One who my Dallas office likes and respects. That's you."

"You'll find a reason to fire me." It was her greatest fear. She'd lost too much to risk again.

His eyebrows knit together. "I hate the fact you think that. Why would I do that? If you worked as well as you did this week, I would have no reason to ever entertain the idea." He named a salary that made her straighten. "I'll guarantee a severance of one year's salary if something does come up. Will that be enough to convince you I mean what I say?"

Allie pounded her sippy cup on the high chair tray, the thumping noise making Rachel jump. While she had her pride, she also had her limits. She wasn't stupid—she couldn't afford to turn this offer down. She needed the money.

Oakley used a nearby burp cloth and wiped Allie's chin. "There you go," he told her daughter. Allie reached her arms toward him, and since he was finished eating, Oakley unbuckled her and set her in his lap. The picture was so perfect and heartwarming that Rachel had to blink multiple times to be sure she wasn't dreaming. Why did Oakley have to be so darn perfect? She'd loved working for him. He seemed nothing like his awful father, and it was clear Allie trusted him. Her daughter didn't warm to everyone.

"Make the offer to Jenny and put everything you've

said in writing. Once that's done, she and I will discuss it and get back to you."

"Consider it done. I'll do whatever it takes to get you to accept."

"I'm leaning that way..." she admitted.

His megawatt smile was enough to make her want to follow him anywhere. "Once you see what I offer, I'll expect you at the office by noon tomorrow. Is that doable? Do we have a deal?"

"If I accept, yes. Deal." When he reached forward to shake her hand, Rachel swore tingles ran up her arm. If the way his eyes darkened was an indicator, he'd felt those sparks, too.

"Good. I'm gonna head out as I assume this little one needs to get to bed soon." He closed the lid of his takeout container.

The word *bed* caused a shiver to run through Rachel. What would it be like to be in bed with Oakley? He'd worn casual clothes today, but his outfit accentuated his lean and muscular frame. Naked, he had to be magnificent, which was a thought she *shouldn't* be having. Was she wise to go back as his admin? But what choice did she have? She had to make the rent. "Yes, it's her bedtime soon."

He passed Allie to Rachel and stood. Thankfully Allie didn't cry. Instead she gazed at Oakley in pure adoration. Rachel couldn't blame her. Oakley put his used napkins and plasticware in the trash can. Careful of the hole in the plastic, he removed the bag. "I'll take this out when I go. Dumpster's out back, right?"

The gesture touched her. "Yes, but then you'll have to walk back around the building to reach the street. I can do it." She assumed he had a car parked nearby so he could drive home. He lived on the outskirts of town. She'd seen the address.

His grin was the stuff of legends, and he directed its full force at her. "Ah, no big deal if it saves you the trip downstairs. I'll see you at noon tomorrow." With a dip of his chin, he took the trash bag and showed himself out. Rachel locked the door behind him and put a new bag into the trash can. She finished tidying the kitchen and readied Allie for bed. Then she turned off the light and went back into the living room and sat on the futon couch that also doubled as a spare bed if needed. She grabbed her phone and dialed. Jenny answered immediately. "What's up?"

A weird sense of giddiness filled Rachel, one she didn't want to examine too closely. Oakley wanted her and was willing to pay big-time to keep her. "Well," she began, "you're not going to believe who just dropped by."

She'd said yes. Oakley thanked his lucky stars as he climbed out of his car and handed the keys to the valet. He'd been driving home when his sister Cheyenne had texted, and after such a crazy day, he'd taken her up on her suggestion of meeting for a drink. He'd turned around and headed for The Green Door, a speakeasy in the Emerald Ridge Hotel. With the hotel having a variety of other places, such as Captain's, Cucina and the Emerald Ridge Café, the Green Door was a hidden gem. To enter, one had to ask for the password at the front desk. After getting that, he went down the hall and entered through a nondescript door with green molding. Once inside the five-by-five antechamber, he picked up the handset, spoke into the receiver and then someone buzzed him through an actual door painted an emerald shade of green.

The speakeasy itself was dimly lit with warm golden

lamps and brass sconces. A bar ran along one wall, and the others displayed an eclectic collection of framed photographs and vintage memorabilia. Rich emerald-green velvet armchairs and a deep brown leather sofa surrounded small brass tables, and these created various intimate seating areas. Oriental-style area rugs in jewel tones defined various spaces, while flickering, flameless candles added ambience. Low conversations hummed, and he found Cheyenne texting on her phone, cocktail on the table in front of her.

"Hey," he said. He bent down and kissed her forehead before dropping into the armchair perpendicular to the love seat on which she sat. "Thanks for suggesting this impromptu get-together when I called."

She sipped some of her martini. "Why not? I'm right upstairs and wanted to get out of my room following a conference call I had about the wedding."

"The one you still plan on attending?"

"Hence the martini. At least I'm not driving." As part of her relocation to Emerald Ridge, his twenty-six-year-old sister was staying in a suite on one of the upper levels.

"That rough?"

"One way to put it." She lifted the lemon drop martini and took a sip. "I'm glad you're here. Better to drink with you than alone, and..." She let the rest of the thoughts go in a resigned exhale. "I keep reminding myself they're my friends and that the bride is one of my best friends, even if it doesn't feel like it since she asked me to step down as a bridesmaid."

If it had been up to him, Oakley would have cancelled attending and told the bride to take a hike. The wedding was in St. Thomas, and Cheyenne would travel to the Virgin Islands at her expense. Even after being asked to step down from the wedding party, she'd insisted on going. Oakley hated that his sister suffered. Her ex had dumped her a few months ago, and since said ex happened to be the groom's best man, the bride had clearly lost this round to her fiancé. Cheyenne had been dumped twice, once by her ex and then by the bride.

"Well, you look great, and he'll be sorry he lost you," he said. He reached for the menu. "You'll be the best-looking one there."

"Minus the bride." She fingered the thin stem of the glass.

"*Including* the bride," Oakley insisted, for his sister was a curvy, petite blonde who often didn't realize how pretty she was.

"I know she feels terrible," Cheyenne said, proving she also had the biggest heart of all the siblings, which is why it hurt him that the bride had dissed Cheyenne this way. Had it been Oakley, he would have already exorcised the best friend from his life, same as he had his cheating ex-wife. But not his sister. She thought the best of everyone.

This was one reason she was so good as a volunteer in the geriatrics department at Emerald Ridge Memorial Hospital. She had a heart of gold. After a stint in the NICU, she assisted with the comprehensive care for those sixty-five and up. While she figured out her next steps career-wise, she'd discovered she had a particular affinity for senior care. Oakley hoped it worked out for her. As he ordered a cocktail from the roving server, he wished there was something more he could do for his sister.

"Tell me more about the guy you found on the riverbank," Cheyenne urged. "You were kind of vague when we chatted yesterday before everyone got online with us."

"Yeah. Dad actually saw him first." Oakley filled her

in on the details, including Clemons's rifling through the man's pockets. "Crazy. Big gash on his head. We have no idea what the stuff in his pockets meant."

She leaned forward. "I shouldn't tell you this, but I know you won't violate privacy laws. The ER docs had to race him to surgery. I left before I found out the results."

"I hope he's going to be okay. I feel a little protective since I found him." And also because his father had read the letter and showed Oakley a photo that had given him the strangest sense of déjà vu.

"There's more." She scooted forward and waited while the server delivered his smoked old-fashioned. She lowered her voice, and Oakley strained to hear. "My friends told me he didn't have any ID on him. No one knows who he is. He's in the system as Johnny Doe."

"Really? That's what the cops said when they were at the scene, but I thought they would have identified him by now."

"Nope. He's still unconscious." She eased back. "Calling him Johnny Doe is better than Patient Alpha. Sounds more personal. I could text someone and get an update, if you want."

Oakley sipped his drink. The bourbon warmed his chest. "Nah. Let's leave it be for now. Maybe I'll go visit him tomorrow. I'd like to check on him and see how he's doing."

"If you wait until afternoon, I could meet you," Cheyenne suggested. "Maybe I can help, since I do have access to the ICU floor. That's where he's been moved."

"That's a great idea. And afternoon is fine. Let's say after 1:00 p.m.? I want to make sure my admin shows at noon."

Cheyenne waved off the server's offer of another martini and let him take away the empty glass. "Why wouldn't she show? You said she was great the last time we talked and that you were pleased with her work."

"Why? Because of our father." He quickly explained about the lawsuit.

Cheyenne leaned against the back of the couch and crossed her ankles. "Wow. You didn't mention that earlier."

"I was still processing it. What are the odds? Does everything our father touches have to come to ruin?"

As Daddy's girl, Cheyenne was the one who was always quickest to defend Clemons, and she didn't fail to rise to the occasion now. "It's a terrible coincidence, but it's not Dad's fault."

"Cheyenne, even you can agree that he didn't need to level a hundred thousand dollar lawsuit against a single mother whose baby puked. Come on, sis. You must admit that's going a step too far."

To his irritation, Cheyenne once again jumped to Clemons's defense. "I'm sure he had his reasons. He's not without his flaws, though. Even I can see them. But surely he wasn't simply being cantankerous. He wouldn't do that."

Oakley chose not to disillusion her. His father had rifled through an unconscious man's pockets. And he'd almost bankrupted Rachel. Oakley wished that his baby sister wasn't so naive at times. But, since Clemons was their father, he didn't belabor the point by reminding her about the returned bottles of wine or the haircut their dad had refused to pay for. She'd simply tell him to suck it up where their dad was concerned, which was what the siblings often did, if only to honor their late mother. Oakley didn't like doing it.

Instead, he shifted the conversation back to Rachel.

"Because of him, I had to pay a pretty penny to get her to agree to work for me again. I went to her place to apologize. She's got a nine-month-old daughter, so now I'm paying for childcare, too."

"I love babies," Cheyenne gushed. "Is her daughter cute?"

"Adorable. I got to hold her." A smiled tugged at his lips. "You'd love Allie. Rachel's raised her well. She's a good mom."

"She must be something. You didn't even chase your last admin when she said she wasn't moving from Dallas."

"Susan was also sixty and ready to retire, so no matter how much money I offered, it wouldn't ever be enough. She was done. I'm hoping that Rachel and I can work together for a long time—she's that good," he admitted. "People in my Dallas office like her already, and it hasn't even been that long. She won them over that fast."

Cheyenne leaned slightly to the left, tilted her head and studied Oakley. "High praise indeed. And you like her, too."

He gave a nonchalant shrug that seemed forced. "Why wouldn't I? She's my admin. It's a two-person office. We have to get along."

Cheyenne puckered her pink-stained lips as she called his bluff. "I meant that you *like* her, like her."

"I do not."

His denial came too hard and too fast. His sister straightened and pushed some of her long hair behind her ear. "Liar."

He tried another tactic. "Look, even if I thought she was attractive…" Nope, he was not going down that path, especially since he did think Rachel was attractive. "Even if I did," he tried again, "I'm not mixing business and pleasure. That's what my first Emerald Ridge admin wanted, and we all saw how that worked out. I had to fire her because of her advances." The memory made him shudder.

"I've been through the same seminars as you have. If it's mutual, and you are transparent with HR, what's the harm?"

"The harm is, I lose an admin who rivals the one I had in Dallas. And thanks to Dad, I almost did. Besides, she's always talking to someone named Taylor. Sounds like a boyfriend." He didn't explain how Rachel's voice would change, becoming even more intimate and friendly while talking to this Taylor person. Just then, his phone beeped. The text was a reply from the employment agency. Jenny had told him she was meeting with Rachel in the morning to review the paperwork and get the new terms into writing. She'd send him an electronic file to sign around 10:00 a.m.

"Good news?" Cheyenne asked.

"Yes. It seems my admin accepted my offer. She'll be returning to work."

His sister beamed at him. "Then I can't wait to meet her and see pictures of her adorable child. And who knows, maybe Taylor is just a friend."

"I doubt that." Besides, as much as he already liked Rachel, her having a boyfriend would keep things professional. He did not poach, *ever.*

"Let's say it is. If so, maybe a single mom and a baby could be exactly what you need in your life. You'd get a premade family. Besides, your love life is pretty dead, and you thought you'd have your own kids by now."

Oakley scowled. "What did I just say about mixing business and pleasure and some dude named Taylor?"

"Oh please," Cheyenne scoffed, in a show of what Oakley considered more of her naivete. "Look, just because you got squashed like a bug by an ex-wife who betrayed you with another man and complained you were too focused on work, that isn't a reason to stop dating. Your love life is flatter than part of the Texas Panhandle. If not Rachel, you should find someone else. You can get on one of those apps."

"That's not happening." Oakley wished he hadn't finished his old-fashioned. He shook the glass and the square ice cube rattled. "And let me remind you, even if I *did* like her, she doesn't trust me. And my own trust level is pretty low. Maybe this is all a ploy to pay our father back through me."

"Really?" Cheyenne stared at him. "Should I remind you that she was the one who quit and you're the one who chased after her?"

"True. It was an idiotic thought," he admitted—one that he'd immediately dismissed the moment it popped into his head. "No. She's not like that. I know that for sure." It was a gut feeling, an instinct, and one he did trust.

Besides, he'd seen her tiny, crammed apartment with the stacked boxes and noticed her shock when he'd arrived carrying food. This wasn't a con he had to worry about. Plus, Jenny ran a legitimate business, which she wouldn't risk. "As I said, Rachel barely trusts me, and I was out of line before. She isn't faking anything. Remember, I have to get things in writing in order to get her to come back and work for me."

"As long as she signed an NDA."

"She did that when she first accepted employment." He sucked the last remains from his glass and set it on the table in front of him. "No, I'm not worried about her. I'm more interested in Johnny Doe."

Speaking of trust issues, Oakley didn't quite believe the fact that his father didn't know the man or didn't have some sort of connection to him. The incident with Rachel had him on guard where his dad was concerned. One thing about Clemons—drama always followed in his wake like flies to honey.

Finished with their drinks and the bill settled, Oakley walked his sister as far as the elevators to the upper floors. She'd been looking at condos along the river, near where he'd found the injured man, but she hadn't decided what she wanted to purchase.

"Thanks for meeting me for a drink. I needed this," Cheyenne said. She gave him a hug.

He kissed her cheek. "Me too and anytime. And, sis? Don't let your so-called friends get to you. You're doing them a favor by still going to the wedding. I'll see you tomorrow at one."

He waited until the doors closed and the only thing he saw was his own image reflected in the shiny brass. He left for home, which was a rented townhouse in a luxury complex. He'd chosen the place because of its view of the river. He drove toward the edge of town. Tomorrow Rachel would return. He'd also find out more about the mystery man, Johnny Doe.

And hopefully, if he was lucky enough, after that life would go back to normal. As for his interest in Rachel, it was nothing he couldn't squash. He had too much to lose if he didn't.

Chapter Four

The next morning, even though she was sitting across from Jenny and had no reason to be anxious, Rachel stilled her tapping foot and jiggly leg. She had to calm her nerves. "Well?"

Jenny peered intently at her computer screen. "Everything looks to be in order." She gave Rachel a smile. "It looks good."

"Are you sure?" Rachel leaned forward, the casual dress she wore bunching under her thighs. "I can't leave anything to chance. Too much is at stake." She'd tossed and turned all night worrying that this was a Venus flytrap. Pretty looking, until you got closer and discovered it was deadly.

Jenny clicked the mouse. "I'm printing the agreement out so you can sign it. It's everything you told me, which is what I discussed with Oakley first thing this morning. I worked with his HR department the moment they logged in." Jenny clicked again before swiveling. "I want you to read it thoroughly because if you agree, I need you to sign it. Once you do, I'll send it back over and you'll head to the office." She reached for the papers on the printer. "Here."

Using the printouts, Rachel began reading the contract. Everything Oakley had promised her was there, from the salary to the health insurance and day care benefits. She still had a probationary period of forty-five days, but after that she'd be a permanent employee with company-paid life insurance and disability coverage.

"I also got you that appointment I told you about at the Emerald Ridge Early Childhood Center," her friend said. "They think they'll be having an opening in the infant room because one of the families might be moving, but they don't have a conclusive answer. Once you tour, you can jump to the front of the wait list. I at least managed that as promised."

"Wow—this is incredible! A miracle. I feel as if I should pinch myself. Are you sure I'm not dreaming?"

Jenny laughed. "No dream. This is real. I'm happy for you, Rachel. You stood your ground and got an even better deal. And on top of that, he gave me a second commission for the trouble."

"He really is a generous man," she said. Once she got a few paychecks under her belt, she'd have enough money to get her car the long overdue service it needed. Living downtown meant she could walk to work, but she'd have to drive to the childcare center, and she'd also need transportation for errands. "This offer means everything."

"It does," Jenny agreed. "He reassured me his father would not bother you. I knew I liked the guy when I first met him during our initial visit after he hired my firm sight unseen. He's clearly got good taste since I'm the best at what I do."

"You certainly are." Rachel began signing the papers. When done, Jenny scanned them in.

Her friend glanced at her computer screen. "Great, I've got it and it looks good. I'm emailing you a copy and I'll file these. You're set. You're good to go back to work. Better yet, since you have a little time, go celebrate by getting a mani-pedi or have someone blow out your hair. While most people make appointments, The Style Lounge takes walk-ins. It's on the way. You should pop in."

"Actually, I do have the time..." Rachel had almost two hours before she had to be at the office. She'd eaten a late breakfast, so she wasn't hungry and wouldn't need lunch. She'd also packed a snack for later.

"When did you treat yourself last?" Jenny prodded.

"Forever and a day ago," Rachel admitted. Doing her hair was a luxury.

"You need to go. In fact, I know the owner, Sofia Fortune, so I'll call ahead and tell them you're coming."

"Thanks. I appreciate it." She hugged Jenny goodbye and took a short stroll to the salon. When Rachel arrived, she found that Jenny had already paid for both a haircut and a mani-pedi, including the tip.

"She said it's because she got paid twice," Sofia said as she directed Rachel to the shampoo bowls. She draped a cape over her and leaned her back, then made a tsk-tsking sound. "You're lucky I'm here today. You have more split ends than the frayed end of a rope."

"Thanks, I think?" Given the precarious state of her finances, she couldn't remember when she'd had her hair cut last. As she usually wore it straight or in a ponytail, it hadn't mattered. Once she'd been jobless, having a routine professional cut was a want, not a need. Not when she had to buy diapers and formula for Allie.

Sofia washed her hair, including an invigorating massage, before she added the conditioner. Once shampooed, an assistant led Rachel to a chair. Sofia caught Rachel's gaze through the mirror. "Trust me," she said before she spun the chair around. A few minutes later, Rachel saw pieces of her dark hair hit the floor. When done, the stylist grabbed a dryer and blew out the strands. "Ready for the reveal?" she asked.

"Um, sure?" Rachel found herself nervous.

Sofia spun her back around, and Rachel gasped. Sofia had taken inches off the length, and the strands fell to right below her shoulders. Instead of straight hair with blunt ends, the layered bob had face-framing layers. Sofia had also added volume to Rachel's hair and the soft waves flipped outward at the ends where they danced along her collarbones. "It's wonderful," Rachel said, feeling happy tears well up in her eyes. How long had it been since she'd felt pretty? *Forever.*

"Thank you. I really appreciate this."

"Come back and I'll add some highlights and lowlights. Yours are natural, but we can bring them out more. Make them really pop."

"I will," Rachel promised. She'd have to learn to create this look at home. She'd need a big round brush, and she made a mental note to add that to her shopping list.

"Perfect. We'll make the appointment for six weeks from now," Sofia said, and Rachel added her next haircut and color to her phone calendar.

She felt the stares of people as she entered the office building, but she could tell their second glances were complimentary. She smiled as she saw her reflection in the elevator. Amazing how a simple haircut could make one feel so good. She practically floated down the hall to the offices of the Fortune Rodeo Corporation. She paused, drew a deep, reassuring breath and reached for the door handle.

Oakley stepped through his office door as she opened the main door. His eyes widened in appreciation before they shuttered into neutral. The fact he'd clearly liked what he saw made her suddenly feel shy. Her reaction to his perusal wasn't from nervous worry, but rather because, for a brief moment, he'd seen her as a desirable woman. She'd felt the zing travel between them, the sensation of his appreciation settling deep in her bones.

"New haircut?" he asked.

"Yes. I was at The Style Lounge. Jenny treated me. She said you paid her extra."

"I did. Seemed she deserved it for all the work she had to do." He paused. "Is it okay if I say your hair looks good and that I like it? I don't want to make you uncomfortable."

"It's okay." Rachel reached to touch her hair and instead jerked her hand down. In order to keep it looking good, Sofia had told her not to run her fingers through it as was Rachel's nervous habit. "It's been a while since I could afford to get it cut, so it's a new style to me, too. Allie's too little to care what I look like, so I haven't worried about it."

"The new cut suits you." Oakley's voice was huskier than usual. He coughed slightly. "Sorry. One question before we begin. That photo you opened yesterday…it's sitting on the bookshelf in my office. Is that going to bother you? If it does, I'll take it home."

The gesture created what could only be described as all the good feels. That he would consider removing a photo of his family just to make her feel comfortable—one containing his late mother—spoke volumes as to Oakley's outstanding character. Her estimation of him rose even further.

"No. Leave it. It was the shock of seeing it that got me.

But you and I worked things out and it's a picture of your family. I'll be fine."

His forehead creased. "If you're certain. If you change your mind, you have to let me know."

"I will." She set her oversize purse on her desk, reached inside and removed the plastic container containing carrots and hummus.

Oakley frowned from where he leaned against the doorframe. "That's all you're having for lunch? That's not a meal."

"I had a late breakfast. You'll see me bring a much larger lunch tomorrow."

He wasn't convinced. "I'm holding you to that. You're a mom. You must keep up your strength." As if realizing he'd entered personal territory again, he straightened and gestured. "Shall we? Say five minutes? Is that enough time for you to get settled?"

"Five minutes is fine," Rachel replied. She went through a door she'd first thought led to a closet but actually led to a private lounge with a kitchen and bathroom.

"Perfect." With that, Oakley strolled into his office. He left the door open, and soon Rachel joined him. They sat perpendicular to each other at a small four-person table, and Oakley pushed some documents in her direction. "These are the new contracts we were negotiating for the rodeo showcase in Lubbock and..."

He explained the details, but Rachel found it hard to focus. She instead noted how his firm fingers held the pen. Her gaze traced the light blond hairs covering his muscular forearm until they disappeared under the rolled-up shirt sleeve. A hint of aftershave or cologne tickled her nose, the scent divine. Had he worn that before? Surely she would have noticed.

Or was she simply hyperaware? He'd been in her apartment last night, after all. But now the dynamic had somehow shifted, becoming more intimate and personal, as if they'd run through a gauntlet together. Working this closely, in a two-person office, things were bound to grow chummier—yet the more he spoke, the more she saw his integrity and business ethics shine through. She found herself softening toward him, and not because he'd paid her more.

Because the truth was, she genuinely liked that he cared about his company and his employees.

"Hello?" a voice called as someone entered the office. "Oakley?" A blonde came into the doorway. She was petite and curvy, and she had a wide smile. "Here you are." Her gaze darted between Oakley and Rachel, and Rachel could see all the assumptions the woman made cross her face. "You must be the new admin. Oakley told me about you last night."

"I am." As Rachel rose, she realized she'd be freaking out if she hadn't seen the woman before; she was one of the women in the family photo. "You must be one of Oakley's sisters."

"I'm Cheyenne." She came forward and shook Rachel's hand. "I'm the youngest and Oakley's favorite." She winked, then her tone gentled. "He told me what our dad did. Clemons has been somewhat adrift since our mother died. I'm sorry you were affected."

Understatement of the year, but Rachel nodded rather than correct her.

"He needs a hobby," Oakley added, taking the liberty he could as a sibling. Cheyenne ignored the dig. It was clear she adored her father.

"It's why we got him a cat," she explained patiently to

Rachel. "Anyway, it's nice to meet you, and I hope you give this guy another chance. He's the oldest boy in our family, and he's been the best big brother. You can't go wrong working for him."

"You don't need to try and sell me." Oakley's embarrassment came through in his gruff tone. "We're work colleagues."

"Exactly." Rachel nodded. She couldn't resist teasing her boss with a little dig of her own. "I'm paid to like him whether I do or not."

"You really know how to wound a guy." Oakley feigned being stabbed in the heart.

"You'd do wise to remember it," she added, grinning. Remembering they had an inquisitive audience who was staring at them openly, she sobered. She didn't want Cheyenne to get any wrong ideas. She and Oakley were employer/employee, nothing more. "I'll get to work on these contracts."

"Thanks." Rachel expected that to be all, but Oakley kept speaking. "I'll be gone for a while. An hour? Maybe two? Cheyenne and I are going to the hospital to check on the man who was injured along the riverbank."

"Jenny told me about that," Rachel said. "He must have been terrified. You know him?"

"No, he was unconscious when my dad and I found him."

"You *found* him?" Rachel hadn't heard that detail, probably because she'd quit in a huff and gone home.

Oakley ran a hand through his hair, and Rachel resisted the urge to do the same. "Yeah. Cheyenne volunteers at the hospital, and I want to check on him myself."

"You should. You discovered him and stepped in to

help. It's natural to want to find out how he is," Rachel encouraged.

"Hopefully the staff has more information," Cheyenne said, her curious gaze darting between Rachel and Oakley. "Yesterday they didn't even know his name. He's in the system as Johnny Doe, last I heard."

"Go," Rachel urged, seeing that Cheyenne was waiting for her brother while Oakley hesitated, his attention still fixed on Rachel. He opened his mouth, and she knew he was about to ask if she was certain. "I'll see you when you get back. I need to call Chad in Dallas, that is, if you want these contracts done," she told him.

His features softened as he trusted she meant what she said. "Good. I'll see you later and explain what I find out about the patient, and you can tell me about the contracts."

"Sounds good." Rachel placed the papers on her desk and took a seat in the most comfortable office chair she'd ever had. The door closed behind her boss and his sister. She started her computer and watched as it loaded.

Then she flattened her palms on the surface of her desk. She spread her hands in opposite directions, as if attempting to wipe away yesterday's drama and cleanse the smooth surface. But her attempt to desensitize and restore calm failed. She had far too much awareness of Oakley as a man to be comfortable. But she was a professional and had made a commitment. Oakley had nothing to worry about. She would be here when he returned.

Chapter Five

"You didn't tell me your administrative assistant was so pretty," Cheyenne remarked as Oakley parked his SUV in the hospital lot. "I loved the dress she was wearing, didn't you? Such vibrant colors. I wonder where she bought it? I'll have to ask her."

"No idea." He prayed his new admin didn't have more clothing like it, for if she did, that might be his undoing. Rachel had been wearing a bold floral pattern featuring blues and greens. The dress was perfectly respectable for the office, with the loose skirt landing at her knees. But he'd been unable to help noticing how the bodice had showcased her breasts. The cap sleeves had directed his attention to her lithe arms. And her hair? Whatever the stylist had done should be outlawed. Oakley had had the sudden urge to reach both hands into Rachel's long, silky locks and feel how soft the strands were, all while kissing a mouth that featured no adornment but a swipe of clear gloss. She wasn't wearing makeup either. She was a natural beauty with a siren's call. He found her *irresistible.*

Which would be a problem if he didn't get his libido under control.

"She was nothing like I'd thought she'd be," Cheyenne said as they walked toward the main entrance. "I liked her."

"I like her, too," Oakley admitted. "So does everyone in the Dallas office."

"Oh, I can see how you liked her." Cheyenne gave him a playful bump on the shoulder. "You couldn't take your eyes off her, and, well, you two appeared pretty tight when I walked in."

"We were going over the contracts."

Cheyenne waggled her eyebrows. "Uh-huh, if that's what they're calling it these days. Then again, you're so ancient, you probably haven't seen chemistry since the Stone Age."

Oakley usually let her ribbing roll off his back, but since this one hit a little too close to the mark, he pushed back in exasperation. "Cheyenne, we work together."

Moments later, Emerald Ridge Memorial Hospital loomed above them, and Oakley let out a huge sigh of relief. As far as he was concerned, they'd arrived in the nick of time, because it nipped any further discussion on Rachel in the bud.

Thank goodness, too, because any more talk about this supposed chemistry between the two of them was *not* a good idea.

The doors to the hospital's main entrance slid open, as did the next set, as they went through the entry vestibule. He followed Cheyenne to the information desk, where a volunteer in her mid-fifties greeted her warmly since the two knew each other.

"We're here to see Johnny Doe," Cheyenne told the woman.

Oakley expected the receptionist to push back by citing health care privacy or something. Instead she began typing on her keyboard. "Well, as no one else has come forward to claim him, you two are probably the closest thing he's got to having people who care."

"Really?" Cheyenne leaned her elbow on the divider. "No one else?"

"No visitors, except for the police. They left about an hour ago. I overheard them talking about the fact he has amnesia. They have no idea who he is, and neither does he."

"That's crazy. Wow." Cheyenne's lips widened into an O of surprise. "He must have hit his head harder than we originally thought."

She and Oakley put on their visitor badges and headed for the elevator. Johnny Doe had been moved post-surgery to the intensive care unit. "Don't worry, I have access here, too. Besides, you found him and helped him. Maybe seeing you will jog his memory."

"I might have seen him when I was walking to the restaurant to meet our dad," Oakley said. "I passed tons of people, so I can't be certain."

"If you did, and he remembers you, that might really help him get his memory back." Cheyenne paused as the elevator doors opened.

They stepped out and approached the nurses' station. Since Cheyenne knew everyone, Oakley let her do the talking, listening as the injured man's nurse told them that Johnny had regained consciousness briefly after his emergency surgery for an epidural hematoma in his left temporal lobe.

"He has no idea who he is, or how he ended up on the riverbank," the nurse told Cheyenne.

A buzz sounded at her desk, and she raised a finger to call into the room and then dispatched an orderly to help a patient to the restroom. "All of that from a gash?" Cheyenne asked. "Oakley found him. Said it looked bad."

The young nurse nodded. "Took sixteen stitches to close. The CT scan also showed a contrecoup injury affecting the right temporal lobe, which we believe is causing him to have amnesia yet still allows him to have the capability for speech."

"I don't know what that means," Oakley muttered.

"The fall on the left side of his head caused the initial hematoma, while the brain's momentum resulted in a contrecoup injury to the right temporal lobe," the nurse explained.

"In other words, it means that when he fell on the left side, Johnny's brain sloshed to the right and hit his skull, causing damage on that side as well," Cheyenne told him. "Johnny has a traumatic brain injury and it's bad. He'll be here awhile."

"At least three weeks, but he won't spend the whole time on this floor," the nurse confirmed.

"Because of the surgery, the staff will monitor him for continued bleeding or swelling in both temporal regions during recovery," Cheyenne added for Oakley's benefit.

"Ah, okay. Makes sense." He found himself impressed by his sister's knowledge, and the easy way she communicated with the nurse. Apparently, she'd learned a great deal in the time she'd been volunteering. They made their way to the patient's room and found Johnny Doe awake and hooked up to monitors. He blinked at them.

"You're not the nurse." Oakley noticed that besides being raspy, the man enunciated his speech clearly.

Cheyenne pressed the button and let the person who answered know Johnny needed someone. "Your nurse will be here in a minute."

"Thanks." The man grimaced, as if speaking had hurt. He appeared to be in a lot of pain, which Oakley figured was par for the course. He didn't want to keep him any longer than necessary. "And you are?"

Oakley automatically stepped forward as if to shake the guy's hand and then thought twice. Johnny didn't appear as if he wanted to move. "Sorry. I'm Oakley Fortune, and this is my sister Cheyenne."

"Fortunes," the man muttered.

"Yes. Oakley's the one who found you." As if she was helping one of her geriatric charges, his sister adjusted his pillow. "There. That looked uncomfortable."

"It was." The injured man coughed slightly, and Cheyenne lifted his water jug and had him take a sip through the bendable straw. He nodded at her when done, and she set the cup back on the over-the-bed table. "Thanks."

"I wanted to check on you, see how you were," Oakley said.

Johnny's blue eyes held his. "Feel like crap." His hand lifted as if to touch his forehead, which was covered in layers of white gauze. On one side, a few tufts of dark hair stuck out. On the other, the surgeons had most likely shaved most of his hair away. "They tell me I hit my head and needed surgery since I was bleeding internally. Do you know what happened to me?"

Oakley explained what he'd seen on the riverbank when he found him.

"Don't remember it or why I was there. No idea who you are, either. Sorry." Johnny winced again.

Oakley kept his smile friendly. "No worries. We thought it might help your memory, seeing me. Guess not."

"Worth a try," Johnny said. "I'll do anything at this point." In obvious pain, he grimaced again.

"Do you still have the letter and the photo?" Cheyenne asked. When Johnny told her he thought the nurse had put them in the closet, she retrieved them and gave them to Oakley. He hadn't had a decent chance to study the items the other day. Unlike his dad, he'd been more concerned with trying to get the man help than solving a mystery. He showed Johnny the picture of the smiling baby, but Johnny shrugged. Then he took the letter out of the envelope, unfolded it and read the letter aloud. "*I think of you often and hope you forgive me.*"

Johnny tried to get comfortable. "No clue what this means. As I said, I have no memory. Not of the fall or how I got here. Sorry."

"Shh. It'll be okay," Cheyenne promised. She offered him more water, which he eagerly sipped. "We're going to help you and we'll figure it out."

Johnny tried to nod, grimaced instead and closed his eyes.

"We should go." Oakley took photos of the items that had been in Johnny's pocket before handing them to Cheyenne so she could return them to the closet.

"Once I get a break during my shift, I'll come back and check on him," Cheyenne said.

Hearing that, Johnny's eyes flew open. "Fortune. You're Fortunes."

Cheyenne smiled. "Yes. We said that earlier. Did you remember anything?"

"Clemons Fortune." Johnny frowned. His eyebrows knit together as if a huge burst of pain had blasted through him. He closed his eyes. "I know that name. But how?"

Oakley wanted that answer, too. "That's my dad. He was with me when we found you."

"Don't remember that," Johnny reminded him. "Why can't I remember?"

"Because your brain has an injury," the nurse said, entering. She scanned her badge to log into the computer. "I've got your medications and we're going to check your bandages."

"Good," Johnny said. "Everything hurts."

"Of course it does," the nurse told him. "You've had a traumatic injury requiring surgery. It'll take a little while to heal."

Since Johnny was preoccupied with getting his meds and neuro checks, Cheyenne and Oakley left the room. "Do you think he knows our dad?" Cheyenne asked. "That would be weird."

Oakley hoped that Johnny Doe wasn't another victim of their father's overzealous legal actions, like Rachel had been. "Dad said he didn't recognize the guy on the riverbank." And while Clemons might be quick to feel wronged and chase justice, whether truly warranted or not, his dad wasn't a liar. Unless that had changed with the move to Emerald Ridge.

"I've got to go visit my patients," Cheyenne said. "Normally my shift is in the mornings, but I said I'd cover this afternoon. Be sure to keep me posted."

"You do the same, sis, especially if he gets his memory back." He kissed her on the cheek. Before they parted, the nurse stepped out.

"We didn't agitate him, did we?" Cheyenne asked the woman what Oakley was thinking.

The nurse shook her head. "No. It's not your fault. He's in a great deal of pain, which is normal following surgery, and he's frustrated because he has amnesia. Healing takes time, and his recovery is compounded by not knowing who he is." She cleared her throat. "But once he's cleared of the effects of anesthesia, and we're certain he can give informed consent, we'll administer a DNA test and allow the police to take and run his fingerprints. That'll most likely be tomorrow. Today he needs to rest. I gave him something to help him sleep."

The nurse left, and they walked back to the elevator bank. Cheyenne pressed both buttons, Up for her and Down for Oakley.

"I'll see if Dad has any idea why our amnesiac might have said his name." He kissed his sister's cheek again and stepped into the elevator when the doors opened.

Oakley couldn't escape the growing unease taking root in his gut. He prayed Johnny's case wasn't another situation where Clemons was suing someone who didn't deserve it. Had he seen Oakley's dad on the promenade? Maybe he'd tripped and had fallen while trying to get out of the way?

Oakley had always had the philosophy that it was one thing to take on a corporation that had failed to protect its consumers, or to receive compensation for the pain and suffering caused by a wrongful motor vehicle accident. That's why people carried liability insurance. However, it was another thing to sue or harass individuals because of things like baby puke or because his dad didn't like the wine. He was becoming more and more convinced that Clemons had filled the hole in his heart, left by his wife's death, with constant complaining and litigation.

Using his car's hands-free function, Oakley called his father and found him at home. "I was at the hospital. Mind if I stop by?"

Once his dad said yes, he called the office. Rachel answered immediately, and he smiled as he heard her voice.

The fact his heart also gave a little flip was nothing to worry about. He told himself he did not "like" her the way Cheyenne insinuated, even if part of him whispered that was a lie. "Hi, Rachel, I won't make it back in today. I have another errand to run first."

"Okay. How was the patient doing?"

He recounted what he'd learned, leaving out the man saying Clemons Fortune's name.

"That poor man," Rachel murmured. "I can't imagine not knowing who I am, much less also being in so much pain. In the meantime, I've got things under control here. I've emailed you the updates from Dallas and sorted your mail."

"Perfect. I'll see you in the morning. And Rachel?" He paused for a second. "I'm glad you're back."

Her voice came softly through the SUV speakers before she disconnected. "Me too."

The smile was still on his face when he arrived at his father's, and Clemons noticed. "Whatcha so happy about? Did the guy get his memory back?"

Oakley shoved his car key fob into his front pants pocket. "Actually, quite the opposite. But he did say your name."

"What? Never seen him before." Clemons grumbled something Oakley didn't quite catch as he followed his father to the great room at the back of the house. He glanced around. Normally his dad's cat would be sunning himself on the couch.

"Where's Mewington?" he asked.

Clemons gestured out the window. "Outside in the catio. Loves it out there. All day he comes and goes as he pleases through that kitty door. Whiskey?"

"Sure." It was technically happy hour, or close enough if

you went to the bars that began happy hour early. Not that Oakley was happy. There were still too many unanswered questions regarding why his father's name had struck a chord with Johnny. He sipped the expensive Scotch and listened to Clemons rant about some new slight. At the right moment, Oakley shifted the conversation back to Johnny Doe. "He doesn't know who he is or anything about the accident. But any idea why he blurted out your name?"

"Like I said—no clue. And I don't recognize him, so I'm certainly not suing him for anything. He best not be trying to pin this on me. Maybe he saw my name in the papers somewhere, about me being a Fortune."

Could his dad have a point? After all, Clemons *had* gotten plenty of press over the years.

"Maybe, though I doubt that he's after you," Oakley said, hoping he was right. If anything, he thought the man might have been trying to get away from Clemons. "You're sure you didn't see him on the promenade?"

"I said no."

"You know, it might be a good idea if you go see him tomorrow. Maybe that will jog his memory, and we can solve this mystery. I can meet you there."

Clemons blanched. "No."

"Dad, the guy knew your name. He has no memory, but he remembered *that* when he's trying to recover from surgery? It doesn't make any sense. Cheyenne said it's weird, and it is. It can't be a coincidence."

"Not going to no hospital," Clemons insisted.

"I know you don't like them after what happened with Mom."

Before he could add a "but," his dad cut Oakley off. "I said no. I hate them. Places of death." Clemons spit out the words before pouring himself another finger of whiskey.

"They're horrible and I'm not doing it. You can't make me. Didn't we have this talk about respect yesterday? I'm your elder, boy. You best remember that."

Oakley hated to press the issue, though his gut was telling him not to ignore it. His dad always seemed to leave a trail of trouble wherever he went, and truly seemed nervous about what his connection to the guy might be. Clemons's refusal came from a place far deeper than hating hospitals after his wife had died in one. That was even more reason to solve this mystery.

"Look, you need to visit him. Get to the bottom of this. I said I'd go with you. Maybe you'll recognize him better now that he's awake and cleaned up. Maybe he's a friend of someone you know. Or a relative."

"Nope." Clemons tucked both his lips under and squared his jaw. "Not happening."

"I'm afraid I have to insist." It was rare that Oakley put his foot down, but he really didn't have much of a choice. "He knows your name. We need to find out why. We moved to Emerald Ridge to get a fresh start. We can't let this mystery derail our status in our new town, not for you, or for me and my siblings."

Clemons harrumphed and folded his arms. Then he loosened them and took another sip of whiskey. He lifted his forefinger and tapped it lightly against the glass. "Fine. We'll go first thing. I don't want this spoiling things for you kids. But this is a big request. You best remember that and show me some respect."

"I will, and I'll make sure the others know the sacrifice you're making." That was only fair. "Cheyenne might even be working. She was a great help today. Her coworkers really seem to like her."

"Why wouldn't they? She's my daughter and she's as

pretty and generous as her mother. You staying for dinner or what? The housekeeper left some meals in the refrigerator."

"Sure. But let me make a call first."

When Rachel got the call from Oakley, she frowned but answered. She had just put Allie in her high chair and her daughter was fingering food into her mouth. She put the phone on speaker. "Hey. Did you not find everything I left on your desk?"

"To be honest, I haven't even been back to the office. I have a big ask, though. I'm at my dad's for an early dinner, and I need to accompany him to the hospital tomorrow."

"Is he okay?" Even though he had sued her, she wouldn't wish Clemons harm. She wasn't that cruel, and she cared for Oakley—as a boss—and he clearly loved his dad.

"He's fine." He lowered his voice. "Johnny Doe has amnesia but for some reason he remembered my dad's name. We don't know why, and neither does he. I want my dad to visit. See if he recognizes him now, or we'll see if maybe Johnny will remember my dad."

"That makes sense. And I'm glad nothing's wrong with your dad."

"Me too. At least not physically."

"Noted." She handed Allie some more cereal and made faces at her. Allie giggled.

"But that brings me to the big request. My dad has hated hospitals ever since my mom died five years ago. Her death is one reason he's, well, the way he is."

Rachel had experienced that firsthand.

"Do you mind if we do tomorrow morning's work tonight?" Oakley asked. "That way, I can accompany him to the hospital. If you agree, I can swing by the office and grab what we need. I'll come to your apartment, of course, so that it doesn't throw Allie off schedule." As if he could sense her hesitation, he added, "I'm also happy to pay you time and a half for the hours…and give you tomorrow afternoon off with pay."

That was more than generous, and her heart gave a little leap at the idea of seeing him. "Okay. We can do that. I'll see you when you get here." She ended the call and glanced around her small apartment. With no idea where Oakley's father lived, or how long it would take him to arrive, she did some fast straightening. She'd taken off her good clothes when she'd arrived home, putting on sweats instead so she could clean, and she raced to her bedroom to find something a little more presentable. She grabbed a dark blue cotton T-shirt dress that came to her knees—it was casual and practical. There was no time for lip gloss or fussing with her hair.

A knock at her door made her start. She opened it to find Oakley standing there, messenger bag on his shoulder and brown paper bag in hand. This one came from the Emerald Ridge Bakery. Whatever was inside smelled divine. "My momma taught me to never arrive empty-handed, especially when I'm asking for a favor."

"Favor?"

"Yes, for asking you to work late tonight." He gave her a grin that made her weak at the knees. "So I brought brownies and sugar cookies. I figured those were soft enough to chew for Allie, if she's allowed any."

"That's very kind of you," she said. "But pediatricians advise parents not to let babies have sweets until they've turned two years old." She plucked the bag from his fingers. “I, however, happen to love both of these and have no such restrictions.”

“Then I’m happy there’s more for you.” Once again, his smile threatened to suck her under, a magnetic force she couldn’t resist. She wanted to bask in its pull and let it draw her in completely. But she’d made that mistake with Allie’s smooth-talking sperm donor. Oakley might be completely different, but he was still a man. One her body wanted. He was also her boss. She’d have to tread carefully, especially since he’d been in her apartment twice. It felt natural and added a layer of intimacy, which was already dangerous because it made her relax her guard around him, as if they were actual friends.

Allowing the smell of fresh baked goods to distract her, she peered into the bag. There were two sugar cookies and two brownies. “Go ahead and take a seat. Allie’s finishing dinner and then I’ll be putting her in her crib for the night.” She removed one of the sugar cookies. It was still warm. She held it out toward him. “Cookie?”

His grin was both sheepish and endearing as he shook his head. “I bought myself one and ate it on the way. Oatmeal chocolate chip.” He winked at her. “What can I say? It’s not one most people like.”

But then he was not like most people, and butterflies flitted in her stomach to prove it. She tried for casual. “Are there any bad cookie flavors? They’re *cookies*.” To calm her racing heart, she took a bite. “Oh, my.”

“Uh-huh. See?”

She had to resist closing her eyes as the buttery and sugary flavor danced on her tongue. “You’re right. This is so good.” She grabbed a small white plate from the cabinet and set the uneaten portion on it. “I can see why you couldn’t wait to eat yours.”

He'd sat at the small table, his big, masculine presence filling the kitchen. She wasn't certain if Allie recognized him or not, but her daughter clapped her hands and babbled as she finished the food on her high chair. Several times she offered Oakley her sippy cup, and he pretended to take a drink before handing the cup back. Rachel's heart swelled at the cozy and cute scene. Oakley had a way with kids. He'd make an excellent father one day. He was the type of man a woman would never have to worry about; he was strong, steadfast, and true.

The kind of man she'd always wanted, but had never found. *Until now?* Perhaps inviting him over had been a mistake. He was her boss and off-limits.

As Rachel lifted Allie from her high chair, Oakley opened his messenger bag. He reminded himself that work was why he was here. He needed to focus. But it was hard, especially when Rachel lifted Allie's hand and waved it at Oakley.

"Say goodnight to Oakley, Allie," Rachel told her daughter. Allie chortled when he grinned and made a funny face. Oakley's heart filled and he waved back. Allie might not be his, but she'd already captured his heart. If he wasn't careful, her mom might do the same.

"I'm going to wash her up and put her to bed," Rachel said. "Once I'm done, I'll get my laptop and meet you in the living room."

"Great. I'll get started organizing the files. Don't rush on my account." He removed his laptop from the bag while Rachel went into the bedroom. A knock sounded on the front door. "Rachel?"

"Yeah, that's Taylor. Can you get that?"

"Sure." Taylor was coming by? Embarrassment washed

over him. He had to remember that Rachel didn't belong to him—she *worked* for him. This cozy scene was an illusion. He went to the front door and opened it, and found himself surprised as no man stood there.

"You're Taylor?" He stared down at a petite, elderly woman with gray hair. He had a full foot or more on her.

"That's me. The question is, who are you?"

"I'm Oakley." He stepped back.

"Isn't it after-hours?" Taylor asked, disapproval evident in her full frown as she entered the apartment.

To Oakley's relief, Rachel came out of the bedroom. She reached for the diaper bag Taylor held. "Hey, Taylor, I see you met my boss."

"I did. Didn't know he'd be having you work all hours of the day or from home."

Rachel set the bag on a side table. "It's fine. He's paying me overtime and giving me tomorrow afternoon off. I'll see you tomorrow morning when I bring Allie over."

"Uh-huh." Taylor left and closed the door behind her. Oakley got the impression she didn't like him much.

"And that," Rachel said, "is my neighbor and Allie's caregiver. She's a bit protective of us."

"I came to that conclusion. I'm surprised, is all. I'm not sure why I thought Taylor was a guy, but I did."

"Oh, no. I'm quite single. After Allie's dad, my ex…" Rachel shook her head. "No use getting into that. No time to date anyway, and men don't want a woman with a child."

"More fool them." For some reason he found himself extremely pleased by this turn of events, and who wouldn't want Allie? She was adorable. Oakley thought he'd have kids by now. And Rachel was a great mom and attractive.

She roused her laptop and logged in from her spot on the couch perpendicular to him. He caught his breath when she tucked her hair behind her ear. He had to remember she worked for him and was off limits, even more so knowing she was single.

"We're in the homestretch for the championship showcases. Where are we with the corporate sponsors?" she asked.

Oakley focused. He'd hired Rachel because of her skills, not because she was beautiful. Either way, she was enchanting.

As they worked on the Fortune Rodeo Corporation's signature event, they fell into a smooth, natural rhythm that he appreciated. While his corporation put on rodeos all over Texas, the one in Dallas was the biggest, and it was the key to Oakley's expansion plans.

"You like rodeo?" Oakley asked during a brief lull. "When I hired you, I hoped you'd be somewhat familiar with the basics of the sport, but clearly you're an expert. You know rodeo inside and out."

Her smile created a warmth he wanted to bask in. "My dad enjoyed it, so he would take me. While I can ride, I never wanted to try competing myself, but I loved watching. I'm partial to the timed events more than the rough stock."

"Really? What, no bull, bareback or saddle bronc riding?" he quipped, handing her some papers.

"Honestly, those events make me nervous for the competitors. That's part of the appeal for the fans, I guess, as so many attend. But it's not me." She set the papers next to her.

"Rodeo is about the skill of the rider. The more dramatic and awe-inspiring, the better. It's why, when I started this company, I wanted to have competitions that attracted the best riders around. Our showcases are more than buckles and the bragging rights. The purse matters as well."

He took pride that the Fortune Rodeo Corporation had extremely generous winnings, which was one reason Oakley had become so successful. He and Rachel spent the next several hours working, ending with a list of items for her to tackle the next day as she liaised with those who worked in the Dallas office.

Oakley stood and stretched his neck. When she closed her laptop screen, he reached his hand out. "Great work tonight."

He instantly realized it was a mistake to touch her when an electric shock ran through his arm as he assisted her to her feet. As if also feeling it, Rachel dropped his hand. "Would you like some coffee? Help me eat some of those desserts you brought?"

He would love to stay, but he didn't need a nightcap, not with his libido on red alert. "Will you hate me if I call it a night? It's late, and I've taken enough of your time. Thank you for the offer, though. Another time."

"Okay." If she'd been disappointed, she hid it well. She stood and made to move around the coffee table.

"Watch out!" His warning came too late. She stepped on one of Allie's wayward toys, tripped and bumped into the coffee table. When she stumbled, Oakley was there to stop her flailing. He moved swiftly, scooping her into his arms and lifting her up and over the table. This put her fewer than twelve inches away from his face. He gazed into her eyes and swore time stopped. "Are you okay?" he asked.

Because one thing was certain—he for sure wasn't.

* * *

Rachel was in Oakley's arms. Big, strong, powerful arms that held her gently. She fought the overwhelming urge to put her hand on the side of his jaw and trace the texture of his five-o'clock shadow. As it was, her fingers splayed against his chest. His lips were tantalizingly close, and she licked her own without even realizing she'd done so, until his eyes darkened with a desire that matched her own. A heady sensation ran through her. Her fingers curled into his soft cotton shirt, a contrast to the hard muscles underneath. "Rachel?" he prompted.

What was she doing?

She came to her senses. "I'm fine. You can set me down." Her words came out strangled, traveling on a slight puff of air. He lowered her to her feet. He didn't release her, but kept his arms wrapped around her lower back until she was steady.

He peered into her face. "You're sure you didn't hurt anything?"

With every nerve ending singing "ooh la la" at being held by him, she tried to make light of the situation. "Just my pride. Stubbed my toe, that's all."

"Let me take a look." He guided her into the chair before moving the coffee table. He squatted down. "The right foot? May I?"

"Uh-huh." She couldn't help but stare as firm fingers assessed the condition of her ankle before moving to gently massage each of her toes. Never had she been so grateful she'd taken Jenny's advice to have a pedicure.

"Pretty color," he said as he noted the red on her toes. Using both hands, he ran his thumbs from her toes to the underside of her foot, rubbing deeply into the arch. The nail tech certainly hadn't given Rachel this kind of attention during the salon technician's standard foot massage. Having not had any male touch in almost two years, if he didn't stop, she'd orgasm simply from his fingers caressing her foot. He must have recognized that, for he released her. "Think you're okay."

If he wasn't her boss, she'd launch herself from the chair and kiss him madly. "That's good," she managed instead. "Thanks for checking."

He rose, and she saw his hands shake, proving he wasn't unaffected. Good. At least she wasn't the only one feeling this awkwardness as they absorbed the implications of an almost kiss.

"It's late. I should get going," he said gruffly.

"And I'm fine," she added. When he moved, she stood unassisted and made sure her dress fell to her knees. "You're welcome anytime. I'm planning on enjoying my afternoon off. The weather is supposed to be lovely and so Allie, Taylor and I will go to the park. As you know, she cares for Allie when I'm at work."

"And it's clear she cares for you, too."

"She does. I got lucky with her as my neighbor. I'm still looking for childcare. I have an appointment and we'll see if it's a good fit or not. No idea when there might be room. Even with Jenny knowing the director, who moved me to the front of the wait list, the center isn't anticipating any openings for several months. The family that was moving is staying put." She trailed him to the door. "Thanks for dropping by."

"Thanks for being so exceptional. For being you," Oakley told her. He hesitated, and Rachel wondered what he was going to say next. But before he did, a cry came through the baby monitor, and he pointed toward the bedroom door. "Go. Allie calls."

With that he was gone, the door closing with a click behind him. Rachel went to check on Allie. She discovered she'd already gone back to sleep, so nothing for Rachel to do but watch her for a few minutes before leaving her be.

She sat on the sofa and touched her lips. She was certain as the sun would rise tomorrow that Oakley had wanted to kiss her as much as she had wanted to kiss him. The thought was crazy, but the signals had been clear. He'd wanted her. She'd wanted him. He could be her dream man.

If only he wasn't her boss.

Chapter Six

Cheyenne was right, Oakley thought as he went to pick up his father and take him to the hospital. He did "like" Rachel. He'd certainly come close to kissing her last night, a fact which had kept him awake. He normally slept like a log, but he'd had the worst case of insomnia, and finally, once he'd fallen asleep, he'd tossed and turned. He'd woken to discover half of his covers on the floor, most likely kicked off while he'd been dreaming. Thankfully, he didn't remember those dreams. He might not get through the day if he did.

As it was, he had a vivid memory of how close his and Rachel's lips had been. It was etched permanently into his brain. Same for the way she had stared at him doe-eyed, as if she wanted to cup the side of his face. He'd felt the undercurrent, the wave of desire so powerful he'd almost been unable to control himself. Somehow he'd managed. He could not lose her as his administrative assistant because he couldn't banish his lustful thoughts or keep his hands to himself. He prided himself on being a man who could control his baser impulses. But when she'd been in his arms, it had been like holding a piece of heaven. He'd wanted more.

Even though Oakley was five minutes early, Clemons

was already outside on the sidewalk when Oakley parked, so he didn't even turn the car off. His old man climbed inside. "Don't want to do this," he said without preamble. "Only doing it for you kids."

"Thank you and good morning to you, too," Oakley replied, waiting until his father fastened his seat belt. Oakley took his time driving, obeying the speed limit as he headed toward the hospital. God forbid they get into an accident and then Clemons had to sue his own son. "Did you sleep well?" he asked.

"No," his dad bit out. "I don't like this. What does this guy want with me? Why did he call my name?"

"I don't know, which is why we're going there to find out. It'll be okay." If Clemons's long dramatic sigh was any indication, Oakley's reassurances hadn't landed the way he'd hoped. "If we're fortunate, Cheyenne will also be there."

He parked and joined Clemons on the pavement. Like most days, his dad wore a white linen suit. He attempted a brave face, but his skin had paled. "Let's do this," Oakley said. "Sooner we do, sooner it'll be over."

Since Cheyenne had added their names to Johnny's guest list, they retraced the route that Oakley and Cheyenne had taken the day before. Clemons grimaced as he stuck the visitor's badge onto his lapel. "This better not leave a mark."

"If it does, I'll pay for the dry cleaning," Oakley offered as he led his dad to the elevator.

However, Clemons shrank back when the doors opened. "Nope. Not going. Forget it. I'm going back to the car."

"The car's locked and it's hot out there. Get in. I know this is hard, but you've got this. We'll be in and out. Promise."

Clemons stepped into the elevator. Two people wedged past, and his dad glared at them. The doors started closing, but Clemons pushed his hand into the gap and the doors retracted. He squared his shoulders and strode onto the lobby floor. He shook his head at Oakley. "Don't care. I'll wait right here. Maybe go to the chapel. The gift store. But you can't force me to do this."

"Dad." Oakley was half in, half out of the elevator, which had started loudly buzzing. People frowned with irritation.

"Go." Clemons turned and stalked off.

Sighing, Oakley stepped into the elevator. He checked in at the desk and when he reached Johnny's room, the door was closed. Through the thin window, Oakley saw the cops were inside. He could always come back. He should probably go find his father.

At that moment, one of the officers stepped out, and Oakley recognized her from the afternoon they'd found Johnny. Her eyes widened in recognition. "I know you. You were on the riverbank."

"How's he doing?" Oakley asked. "I heard he doesn't have family and my sister works here, so I've been back once already to pay him a visit. My dad's downstairs and won't come up. He doesn't like hospitals much."

"Who does? And we don't know anything more than the day we found him. Sadly, he's not Henry Cavill, although there is some resemblance. Probably a good-looking guy when his head's not all banged up. We were taking his statement just now and he doesn't remember anything."

"That's the same thing he told me last night." Oakley gave the officer an update, but he left out the part of Johnny saying Clemons's name.

"We're alerting our news contacts in hopes that once they get the word out, someone comes forward who can identify him. He doesn't fit the description on any missing persons' reports. We're also considering that he may have been the victim of an attack or robbery given the head injury and because he didn't have a wallet on him. We're depending on the public to help. Hopefully, someone saw something. I'm telling you all this because you found him, and because the media may contact you."

Oakley hoped they wouldn't. He could almost hear his father saying, "Those damn reporters. They always need an angle."

Her partner stepped out into the hall. "Done with his fingerprinting," he said. He saw Oakley and gestured toward him. "Why don't you take him back inside?" he suggested. "Maybe seeing him will jog Johnny Doe's memory. I gotta get back to the station. We've got some new intel on that rustling case. Besides, doc says he'll eventually get his memory back, and it's not like our amnesiac is going anywhere."

"Nurse said last night that he'll be in the hospital a few weeks," Oakley chimed in.

"Yeah, we heard that, too." They entered the room and Oakley thought that perhaps it was a good thing that Clemons had refused. Their mother had had similar bandages on her head at one point.

"Hey, Johnny, you remember this guy?" the officer asked, pointing at Oakley.

Johnny stared for a minute. "Oakley," Johnny said. He gave a small smile. "We met last night."

"But before that?" she persisted.

Johnny's smile disappeared as quickly as it had arrived. "No. Never seen him before last night. He came by with his sister. Cheyenne. Wait. They're Fortunes." He grasped for the memory but failed. "Clemons Fortune. Still trying to figure out why I know that name…"

The officer looked at Oakley before glancing back at Johnny. "Do you remember something about Clemons?"

The injured man looked around. "No." He winced as if trying to get the memory to come into focus. "No, I'm pretty sure I don't know the guy. Maybe I know *of* him? I wish I could remember." Oakley could hear the man's frustration and wished he could help him.

"Let me show you a picture of him. He helped rescue you," Oakley said.

He held out his phone, and Johnny stared hard at Clemons's photo. "I don't recognize him…and I just can't remember whether we have ever met before." Then Johnny balled his fists. "Why doesn't my brain work?"

The police officer gave a drawn-out sigh. "I'll be in touch in a few days," she told Johnny. "You tell your nurse if you remember anything. If I find out you're in the fingerprint database, you'll see me sooner."

As if hearing the word *nurse*, Johnny's RN appeared, passing the officer on her way out. The nurse saw Oakley and her eyebrows drew together. She hadn't been on duty the other night. "Who are you?"

"I'm Oakley Fortune. I was the one who found him," he replied. "I visited last night."

"Ah. I heard about that. Johnny said he had some visitors." She lost her suspicious expression. "Johnny, it's time for your pain medicine. Then we'll do the DNA swab. We'll send it to the lab. Thanks for signing the consent forms."

"I need to know who I am," he mumbled. He pressed his hands to his head as if trying to push the memory out.

Oakley watched as the nurse gave Johnny his meds and swabbed his cheek. Then she disappeared with the sample.

Johnny pressed his head deeper into his pillow. “I’m sorry I don’t know you or your dad,” he told Oakley. “But thank you for saving me. I…”

The arrival of the neurologist interrupted whatever Johnny was about to say next, so Oakley took his leave. He found Clemons in the gift shop, and he came out grumbling about the high prices of floral arrangements and teddy bears. “A rip-off, I tell you,” he complained.

His dad at least waited until they got to the parking lot before he began muttering something about suing someone. “Did you find out why the man was calling my name?”

“No. I showed him your photo, and he didn’t recognize you.”

“See?” Clemons declared triumphantly. “There was no point dragging me here at all.”

Oakley let his dad rant the entire drive back to his place.

“Just know one thing,” Clemons said. “If that guy comes after me, I’m suing.”

“I’ll deal with it,” Oakley began, but his dad had already slammed the car door closed and was speed-walking toward the house. Oakley sat with his car idling until his father got safely inside. Then he drove away and after a random thought struck him, he headed back to the hospital. The nurse in the ICU seemed surprised to see him.

“Did you forget something?” she asked.

“No. But until a short time ago, my dad never knew he was a part of the Fortune family. He found out through a DNA test.”

She nodded. “I read about that.”

Nothing like having your family drama aired in public, but then again, that was nothing new when it involved Clemons. This time it had at least been good fortune, pun intended. "Exactly. I want to have my DNA swabbed. That way you can run it in your hospital system against Johnny Doe's DNA and see if there's a match. There has to be a reason Johnny Doe blurted out my dad's name."

"You think there could be a familial connection."

"Maybe. I don't know. I wouldn't think so because my dad was devoted to my mom. I doubt he's my dad's son. But perhaps Johnny could be related to us somehow. We can use my DNA to find out."

"It's not a bad idea. Let me go speak with someone." She rose and walked down the hall, so Oakley went and sat in the ICU's waiting area. A game show was on the television, and contestants were spinning a wheel.

After about twenty minutes, the nurse returned. "Sorry that took so long. I had to ask around, but finally reached someone higher up who agreed it couldn't hurt. You'll need to sign some consent forms and go to the lab since we don't do that here for non-patients. The lab on the first floor is expecting you." She held up a hand, a note of caution in her voice. "But just be aware that our system—and the police's— don't link to those private ancestry websites. If Johnny wants his DNA on one of them, he'll have to make an account and submit it himself."

"Got it."

A short time later, after being swabbed, Oakley was on his way to the office. Since he'd somehow lost the entire morning, he went by Donatello's Pizzeria to grab two slices of pizza for lunch. Arriving at the office, he wasn't surprised to find Rachel gone for the day. Perhaps he'd even hesitated longer than necessary to get back. He wasn't normally this nervous about being in a woman's presence, but after last night… He brushed the thoughts aside. Rachel was his admin. Nothing more. Best to remember that and act accordingly.

He sat at his desk, a green pepper and onion pizza slice in one hand while he thumbed through mail with the other. Then he accessed his email. Rachel had sent him one telling him what she'd accomplished and what he still needed to do, and that she'd see him tomorrow. She'd added a smiley face emoji, which sent a joyous jolt through Oakley.

Darn, he had it bad.

He had to get it together. Yes, he liked her. But he could handle attraction. He'd vowed not to get involved again, especially after the divorce. He couldn't say his cheating ex had destroyed his heart, but she had shredded his pride and left him emotionally battered. No woman yet had slipped past the barriers he'd erected. One or two dates and he was moving on, which was why he rarely dated. Unlike his younger brother, Jagger, Oakley wasn't a one-night-stand type either, which meant it had been forever since he'd had sex. Amazing how he didn't miss it, as the wrong person made sex nothing but a physical release, and he had a hand if it came to that. But with Rachel, the desire was there for real. Being with her would be far deeper and meaningful.

Just a brief note from her had the power to make him feel as if all was right in the world, or as if he could climb the tallest mountain or swim the deepest sea. And yes, he knew that made him seem like a silly teenage cliché. He was reading far too much into it. She might have slipped under his defenses, intentionally or not. Still, he couldn't act on these burgeoning feelings. He could, however, act on others.

He'd seen the state of her apartment. It was tiny and cramped. She needed things for Allie, things she would have been able to pay for, had it not been for his father and his ridiculous lawsuit. Oakley could at least relieve some of the guilt he felt over his father's actions.

He made a phone call to one of his executives in Dallas and within a few minutes had the number for the concierge service the firm often used. When the call connected, he began telling the concierge exactly what he wanted. Once terms were settled, Oakley leaned back and smiled.

He hoped Rachel enjoyed her surprise.

Oakley wasn't in the office when Rachel arrived the next morning. She settled into her desk and spread her hands along the smooth surface. Being Oakley's admin felt good. Right. She'd loved having the office to herself yesterday morning, and having the afternoon off had been fantastic. She'd taken Allie for a long walk in the park and then visited the early childhood center. While she'd liked the place, the director confirmed that the family was staying and didn't have an opening. Because of the age of the infants already in the room, she'd said she didn't expect one for at least six months, even if she moved Allie to the top of the list.

When Rachel had arrived home, she'd told Taylor what had happened. Her neighbor immediately offered to keep Allie daily, and Rachel, insisting she couldn't take any more charity, worked out a fair monetary arrangement that benefited everyone. Until the center had an opening, Allie would stay with Taylor, which suited Rachel just fine. She was actually relieved that her kind-hearted neighbor would be Allie's full-time caregiver. This way, she could go home at lunch to visit her daughter, like she planned on doing today. An added bonus: Taylor had grandchildren of her own, so when her granddaughter visited, Allie would get social time with kids her own age.

The door to the hallway opened. When Oakley came through, Rachel's fingers froze above her keyboard. She took a breath to calm her quickening pulse.

"Hey there," he said, carrying two to-go coffees. He set one on her desk. "Thought you could use a pick-me-up."

"Thank you. That's kind of you." Being generous was one of Oakley's traits. He might be rich, but he wasn't selfish. Instead, he thought of everyone else. She'd seen it time and time again in his interactions with his clients and employees. It was one of the many things she appreciated about him. She found the hazelnut-flavored coffee just the way she liked it. "This is good."

"Because I know a guy," he teased. His dark blond hair caught the light from the overhead fixtures as he hovered in the doorway long enough that she noticed the front crease in his tailored navy slacks. He wore a crisp white shirt, the sleeves rolled up to expose the strong forearms she'd felt firsthand just the night before. His gaze swept the room, and she found herself holding her breath, unable to look away. *He was magnificent.* "How'd Allie sleep? Did she cry long after I left?"

"Oh, she actually went back to sleep immediately. False alarm. It happens."

"That's good. I…um…liked holding her the other night. She seems like an easy baby." He sipped his coffee, which drew her focus to his full lips, so temptingly close to her own.

"She's always been easy. Normally anyway. As you recall, she was screaming when you arrived…"

"Hard to forget," he teased.

This small talk should mean nothing, yet every word felt weighted, as if they were dancing around what had almost happened. "I put those contracts on your desk. When you're ready to sign, let me know and I can witness and sign for you."

"Thanks. I'll go review them now." He disappeared through the doorway and, fingers planted again on the keys, she got back to work. Her sense of alertness didn't fade, even though Oakley stayed mainly in his office. He came out a few times to check in and use their shared restroom and kitchen, but mostly she didn't see him. She had access to his schedule, which today included several conference calls. The Dallas-based championship weekend required tons of attention, and he sent her an email saying not to worry about the contracts as a courier would deliver new ones after lunch. Since he had a luncheon with one of the city council members who was thinking of bringing a rodeo showcase to Emerald Ridge, she sent Oakley a text saying she was taking her lunch an hour early so that she could be in the office while he was gone. That way one of them was there to meet the courier. She got back a thumbs-up.

Since it was a gorgeous day and it didn't take that long to eat a peanut butter-and-jelly sandwich, she strolled at a normal pace instead of her typical "have to catch a plane" speed walk. Allie was at Taylor's, so Rachel went there first. Her daughter raised her arms when she saw her mom, and Rachel scooped her up.

"How's my girl been?" she cooed. She dipped her head as Allie went for some of her hair. "Feisty, I see."

"She's been great. We read a bunch of stories, and she's working on pulling herself up. No steps yet."

"I hope she walks for me first." Rachel blew a raspberry on Allie's stomach. Her daughter laughed, a full and throaty, exuberant squeal. "You take your first steps for me, got it? That's an order."

Allie babbled, so Rachel blew another raspberry into her belly, which elicited another round of giggles.

"Speaking of walking, be careful when you go into your apartment. You had a delivery. I signed for it… I hope that's okay. The driver said everything was paid for already and no balance was owed. He had to make several trips. Since the boxes looked big and heavy, I let him in and supervised."

"I didn't order anything." Nor had Rachel noticed any wrongful charges on any of her credit cards. When she'd been dealing with Clemons, she'd checked the balances online so often it was now a habit. Same with her bank account. Nothing had been amiss. "That's strange. What company was it?"

Taylor named the company, which was a registered and real delivery service. Rachel shrugged. "I have no idea what that delivery is. Shall we check it out?"

Carrying Allie, Rachel went to her apartment and opened the door. There were five huge boxes set on the floor, making the walk inside near impossible. "I did not order this stuff."

But it was her name and address on the shipping labels.

"Open one and see if there's a card or something," Taylor suggested. "I doubt this was one of those scams. It was a private courier. Those are expensive."

"Yeah, but you can't be too careful these days." Using her house key to slice through the packing tape, Rachel broke into one of the boxes. She peeled back the brown packing paper, revealing a set of baby gates. There were also cabinet locks, something she hadn't yet installed but were essential armor as little Allie was already crawling. At least the electrical outlets were done.

"Who sent you all this?" Taylor asked. "What a thoughtful gift."

"No idea yet. Maybe my parents? But I would have thought they'd have texted me. That's what they usually do."

Rachel tore into the second box and found a baby walker, a set of shape sorters and a set of board books she didn't already have. Another box contained clothes and shoes with flexible soles, perfect for when Allie started walking. There was even a Radio Flyer Busy Buggy, along with a grocery cart that doubled as a walker, push toy and role-playing item all in one. It even came with a kid-size coffee cup that fit in a holder.

"Someone likes you a great deal." Taylor lifted the pink stuffed unicorn, which began playing the ABC song when she squeezed its hoof. The other hoof counted aloud. Allie squealed and grabbed the plushie, but it was almost the same size as she was. Taylor set her in the playpen with it and the unicorn began counting to ten. "This is really generous. These are fabulous gifts."

"I'm not done." The next box contained a Playskool Weebles My Smart House, and another had a quilted basket filled with six soft fabric baby dolls. There was even a huge stuffed teddy bear that doubled as a toddler chair.

"I don't even know where I'm going to put all this stuff," Rachel said. She noticed a four-by-six envelope. It must have fallen off when the delivery driver set the boxes inside. She ripped into it to find a card embossed with the name of Emerald Ridge's best baby store. Inside was a printed message: *Noticed you could use a few things. Thanks again for saying yes! Oakley*

"Yes to what?" Taylor asked.

"For the overtime the other day…or maybe for me coming back to work? I told you how I'd quit." Rachel calmed shaky fingers as she put the card back into the envelope. Oakley had again proved how generous and exceptional he was.

Taylor arched an eyebrow. "Was that what you call it? *Working?* I heard him leave that night. It was late. Way after hours."

Rachel's face flamed. "Yes. Work was all it was," she insisted. "He had to meet his father, so we worked an extended day. He came to the apartment since I had Allie. That's why I was off yesterday afternoon."

"I could have watched her," Taylor reminded her. "Having your boss in your home seems like crossing a line."

It would have been if they'd kissed, but they hadn't…

"I didn't mind Oakley being here. It was after dinner with his father. He paid me extra, and I got the afternoon off. He's a fair employer. I could have said no."

"You need to be certain you can set boundaries, especially if needed."

"I can." As long as she didn't throw herself at him or keep thinking about him constantly. "He's not his father."

Taylor nodded thoughtfully. "How's his dad taking it that you're still working for him?"

Rachel hadn't thought of Clemons's reaction. "Now that you mention it, I don't know. I try to avoid anything to do with his dad. Oakley is who matters. I do like working for him."

"Well, he seems extremely grateful that you're back

with him. It's clear he likes you very much if this is how he rewards his employees."

With those words, Rachel's initial euphoria evaporated. Was Oakley doing this for other employees? Or just her? "Taylor, I can't accept these gifts! It's wrong. Unethical. I don't want to be seen as a favorite."

Taylor began stacking the board books. "Why not? It's good stuff. You said no one crossed a line. Can't a boss give an employee a gift if he's not expecting a quid pro quo?"

"He could, if he's doing it for others. I don't know if he is. And no, it's definitely not a quid pro quo." Any desire Oakley harbored for her was matched by her own. He wasn't asking for special favors, and he wasn't harassing her. These gifts were proof of how thoughtful he was. But she could see the optics of the situation and realized how it might look to others. He'd fired his last admin for trying to become Mrs. Oakley Fortune. What would her colleagues in the Dallas office think if they knew what he'd done?

Taylor wadded some of the packing paper and returned it to the box. "If you don't want him to do these things, then you may need to have a conversation with him and establish firm boundaries. If you need me to watch Allie so you can work late at the office instead of at your home, just ask. With enough notice, I can make it work."

"I'm not having you miss your social outings." As for boundaries, she and Oakley had already tried to set some, and then they'd almost kissed the other night, and she'd wanted that kiss. *Desperately.* Was this payment so she'd forget that? No, he wasn't like that. Or was he...? His dad had an ulterior motive for everything and was sue-happy. Rachel's confusion made her head feel light.

Did Oakley still feel sorry for her? Had the few times he'd been in her apartment made him think she couldn't provide for Allie? The thoughts haunted her on the walk back to the office, and she worked on rehearsing what she'd say to him. She didn't want to have to quit again, but she had to draw a line in the sand. She arrived ten minutes early. When she walked in and saw Oakley, all good intentions of approaching the subject logically flew out the window.

"Do you think I'm a charity case?" The words blurted forth, and her cheeks heated.

His expression morphed from confused to indignant. "What are you talking about? Of course you're not a charity case. Where did you get that ridiculous idea?"

"It feels like it. I walked into my apartment, and the place looks like a baby store threw up in there. I can hardly walk there's so much stuff."

He lost the indignant expression. "Great. The gifts arrived. I had a concierge service buy everything. Do you like it?"

"No, I don't like it! Well, I do, but that's not the point." He probably didn't even know what he'd purchased. Rachel didn't know if that made what he'd done better or worse. "Listen, what you did was incredibly thoughtful but also completely unnecessary. You already pay me handsomely. And Allie is nine months old. She doesn't need the best of everything—functional is fine. She won't even remember these things."

"I was trying—"

Even though it was rude, she cut him off. If she didn't, she'd falter. "Just because I'm saving and not splurging so I can get a better place, that doesn't mean that I need your charity. What I want from you is to know that my job is secure, and things like this call that into question."

"Your job is secure. I've told you that." His declaration rang true, but part of Rachel couldn't believe. Was that why she protested too much? Because of the way Allie's baby daddy had treated her and the number he'd done on her psyche? Rachel knew better than anyone how the rug could be yanked out from under her at any time. Oakley could grow tired of her, give her the negotiated severance and put her out on the proverbial street. Then where would she be?

She blinked. She'd been moving while she talked, and she'd backed him up against his desk. Her face flamed as he raised his hands in protest. "Rachel, I like doing things for people. I'm sorry it didn't land the way I'd pictured. I wasn't trying to make you feel like a charity case or someone who needed to be cared for because you couldn't provide for yourself or your daughter. That was never my intention. You are an amazing mom. I wanted to let you know that I see that, see how hard you work. I see you, Rachel, and you're incredible. That's all the gifts were."

She should be thrilled by his admission, but she'd heard those words before, the ones telling her that she was incredible, from her ex. Look how that had turned out. "While I thank you for thinking so highly of me, I don't need you to validate me or my parenting. I don't need you to take care of me. I don't need any—"

Without thinking, she'd raised her finger. She'd pointed it at him, jabbing toward his face like an annoying fly entering his personal space. He wrapped his palm around the digit and snagged her forefinger from the air, drawing her hand downward. She didn't intend to stumble, but she was so shocked by the motion—first by her poking at him and then him grabbing her finger—she simply faltered.

Like the night before, she found herself in his arms and her palm on his chest. Her mouth opened. One of his arms slid around her waist. “Oakley, I…”

“Rachel.” Her name coming from his mouth was a plea.

She had no idea who moved first—did it even matter?—but the first touch of her lips to his was an earthquake. She felt the impact everywhere, from head to toe. This was no gentle kiss or tentative exploration. No slow and steady. This was cataclysmic…a crashing, colliding, molding and melding, born of a sense of desperation that the kiss couldn’t be deep enough, fast enough. Her mouth had to have his, and his hers.

The kiss consumed, elevated and erased everything that had come before as it blazed a new trail. She was standing between his legs as he sat on the desk. His hands were against the nape of her neck and threaded into her hair, the strands of her new hairstyle draped through his fingers. She clutched his shoulders, somehow managing not to collapse as she leaned into him. His tongue touched hers, and then began to explore her mouth. A hand left her hair to cup her bottom, and when he drew her to him, she sensed every inch of his desire.

No words needed to be spoken, almost as if both were afraid doing so would break the spell the kiss wove. They devoured each other, letting their tongues and lips say everything necessary. It wasn’t until Oakley’s phone began trilling that Rachel came to her senses and jumped out of his arms.

By the time he silenced the alarm on his phone, she’d made it into the bathroom and locked the door. She gripped the edge of the sink and stared into her glazed eyes, which had turned a wide, shell-shocked blue. She pressed a finger against puffy, just-thoroughly-kissed lips. What had she been doing? If Oakley hadn't had to get to lunch with the person from the city council, would they have had sex on his desk? So much for creating lines and boundaries. She'd crossed them willingly and would have kept going until reaching a logical—and most likely orgasmic—conclusion. A knock sounded on the door. "Rachel?" He knocked again. "Rachel… I'm sorry, but I have to leave. We'll talk when I get back, okay?"

She drew herself to her full height, turned and threw open the door. Mr. Pure Temptation straightened and searched her gaze. "You okay?"

"That can never happen again," she told him. This time she did not wave a finger. "When you come back, put it out of sight and out of mind. We are professionals. Nothing more. I won't say it was a mistake or that it was unwanted. That would be a lie. But we pretend the kiss never happened. We don't talk about it. We just go on. Understood? I can't work for you if you don't agree."

He gave her a brusque nod. "If that's what you want, consider it done."

"It's what I want."

Maybe. She was torn. But she needed this job, and she released a relieved breath when he let the half-truth slide. "Okay. Done. I want you to be happy, Rachel."

"And I'll keep the gifts, not because I need them, but because it was a nice gesture and I like them." Before he could say anything else, she shut the door in his face and stayed in the bathroom until she was certain he'd left the office.

His business lunch took almost three hours, so by the time he returned it was late afternoon. He smiled at her politely as he entered the inner office, and he went into his personal space and closed the door so he could make phone calls.

She ignored her body's melancholy reaction and shut her eyes. This was what she wanted: distance, space and professionalism. A workspace with no desire. Then why did she feel so awful? She opened her eyes, sighed and got back to work.

Chapter Seven

Located on the penthouse level of the Emerald Ridge Hotel, Captain's was the town's five-star seafood restaurant. It had a fantastic view from its floor-to-ceiling windows, and Oakley and his siblings would have a table overlooking the river. For now, he waited in the bar, glass of bourbon held tight.

He'd kissed Rachel. What had he been thinking? Despite being the only one at the high-top table, he rolled his eyes. He was ashamed of himself. The answer was that he'd lost control. He hadn't been *thinking.* He'd kissed her as if he'd been a drowning man gasping for air. He hadn't been sweet or gentle, but rather rabid with need. It had been the kiss to end all kisses, except that it should have ended before it began. She'd told him no regrets. At least she didn't consider the kiss that had rocked his world a mistake, or acted like it was unwanted. She'd met him with the same ardor, her passion equal to his. Yet somehow that made it even worse. He wanted more.

But how? She'd said it couldn't happen again, and he'd agreed. Even if they declared their desire for a relationship to HR—and Rachel was the type of woman who deserved a committed relationship, not a fling—could it even work between them? While they worked well together, his ex-wife had declared him to be selfish. His business came first.

Since all his siblings were in town, he pushed the matter from his mind. His older sister, Maisey, arrived first and kissed him on the cheek. Like Cheyenne, who arrived next, thirty-five year-old Maisey was petite. Unlike Cheyenne, though, she had long auburn hair and hazel eyes. Avery was petite like her sisters, and Jagger was blond like Cheyenne, but he had the same hazel eyes as Maisey and the same height as Oakley. Of the brothers, he was the playboy, preferring to play the field rather than settle down. Both Oakley and brother Evanston were divorced and considered themselves once bitten, twice shy. They shared that and their blue eyes. Oakley hoped his siblings wouldn't sense anything was amiss, for where Rachel was concerned, Oakley was a mess.

So much so that he'd wanted to cancel the Friday night dinner, but refrained because he figured that would raise more red flags. Especially after the siblings had scheduled it a while ago, and while they talked frequently, their in-person meetups were harder to arrange given everyone's schedules. It would be better once they all lived in Emerald Ridge.

The hostess led everyone to a rectangular table that was angled to provide maximum view. Their server took a drink order, but already having bourbon, Oakley passed. He'd have a glass of wine later with his meal.

"How are your classes going?" he asked Maisey.

"Great! I'm almost done. Soon I'll be certified to be a foster mom. In fact, Poppy Fortune—well, Leonetti now—brought her son in and talked to us this week about the joys of fostering."

"Maisey, that's so wonderful," Cheyenne said.

“You can always practice on mine, Auntie dear,” Avery offered. Her belly was still mostly flat, but she’d told the siblings about her pregnancy. Oakley was excited about becoming an uncle. He loved babies. Which, of course, made him think of Allie and her mom…

“What’s going on with you?” Oakley asked Evanston. Anything to get Rachel out of his head. His brother was a high-profile attorney in private practice who’d been both a prosecutor and a defense lawyer. Surely he’d have something to talk about.

“Just closed on that ranch I had my eye on,” Evanston replied. “I’m renaming it Fortune’s Cattle and going to keep it as prosperous as it’s been. That’s the plan anyway.”

“I’m certain you will make it happen,” Oakley told him.

“The two of you crack me up,” Jagger snorted. “You’re acting like eighty-year-old men with all this talk about settling down.”

“We’re in our thirties, as are you,” Oakley said.

“A recently turned thirty,” Jagger corrected. “Which, despite my old injury, does not mean I’m over the hill like the two of you think your thirties entail. Seriously. When did you both get so lame?”

“Ha ha,” Evanston deadpanned. “It’s called growing up. Something you should try, Mr. Love ’em and Leave ’em.”

“Seems to me you’re the ones getting left.” Jagger grinned, the barb successfully delivered.

“Jagger, apologize,” Cheyenne admonished. “No need to be mean.”

“Wasn’t being mean.” Jagger’s ensuing “sorry” was muffled.

Their server brought their drinks and glasses of water. When she returned and took their appetizer and dinner order, Oakley ordered two bottles of wine for the table. With Avery not drinking, two bottles meant a little over one glass for the rest of them.

"Let's hope these Leonetti vintages are better than the ones Dad sent back," Cheyenne huffed.

"Cheyenne, you know he was just being obstinate like he always is," Maisey said sternly. "There was nothing wrong with that wine. You always defend him."

"I do not." Cheyenne's protest came complete with a pouty lower lip.

"Sure you do," Jagger piled on. "You're the baby of the family. You don't know him like we do."

"He rifled through Johnny Doe's pockets." Oakley's admission made Maisey and Avery gasp.

"He did *what*?" Evanston asked. "And we're just hearing this now?"

"Sorry. Thought I'd told you. Cheyenne knew."

After Oakley explained, Evanston shook his head and said, "Our father is a walking legal disaster."

"He's getting worse," Maisey agreed. "That's why I hoped Mewington would give him something else to occupy his time."

"He did build him a catio," Jagger said. "That cat is super spoiled."

"It's not enough," Avery insisted. "Dad needs more than a cat to talk to."

Oakley shrugged. "Well, he said he had some business ideas…"

"Oh no." Maisey recoiled. "No more of that nonsense. He needs a *hobby*."

Their server was back with several appetizers, and the conversation naturally shifted away from their father. Discussing Clemons often put everyone in a sour mood.

They loved him, but at the same time, they wanted their father to be happy with life and enjoying himself in ways other than complaining and suing people.

"Any idea on who the amnesiac is?" Avery asked after their meals arrived. "You and Cheyenne saw him, right?"

"We did and no idea." Oakley cut into his delicious filet mignon while he told them about giving his DNA and about how Johnny had called out their father's name. "But our dad insists that he doesn't know him."

"Do you believe him?" Maisey asked.

"With our dad you never know," Evanston interjected.

But before Oakley could answer, Cheyenne intervened. "Speaking of not knowing, he hasn't told you about his new administrative assistant."

Oakley glared at his baby sister. Trust Cheyenne to have held on to that bombshell until what she considered the right moment. She'd lobbed the news to draw attention away from their dad's antics.

"What's so special about an assistant?" Avery appeared confused. "She's not the one you fired for harassment, is she?"

"No, she's not and there's nothing going on." Oakley spoke too quickly.

"Oakley likes her," Cheyenne said, giving Oakley a satisfied smirk. "You know that it's true. Look, your cheeks turned pink. I didn't know you could blush."

"I'm not. It's the bourbon."

Evanston scoffed. "Oakley's smart enough to know you don't get your honey where you make your money. It's bad business."

"I hate that saying," Maisey sputtered. "Could you not? It's crass."

"Sorry," Evanston said. "But workplace romances are foolish."

Considering he'd kissed Rachel, and she'd kissed him back, Oakley avoided saying anything more by sipping some wine, which, should anyone ask, had had all the right notes. It was a flawless vintage, same as the bottles their dad had sent back.

"There's nothing wrong with hooking up if both sides agree to it," Jagger said. "Aw. Do you have a crush, Oakley?"

"What are we, in high school?" Oakley shot back. The wine sloshed as he set the glass down with a thump.

Cheyenne tittered. "It's more than a crush. Oakley had to beg her to return."

"Wait, I'm coming into the middle of this story. Someone explain," Avery demanded.

"Fine." Oakley gave in and relayed what had happened. He included everything from how he'd discovered Rachel was the one Clemons had sued to the gifts he'd sent as his appreciation. He left out the kiss. He knew what his siblings would say about that, and he'd never hear the end of it.

"You bought her baby things?" Avery stared, incredulous. "You haven't even bought *me* baby stuff yet."

"And I will, after you've had your baby showers," he said. "It's not that big of a deal. At first, she wasn't planning on keeping them, but now she is. I'd do the same for anyone."

"Have you?" Maisey asked, voicing the same question Rachel had.

Evanston gave a disbelieving shake of his head. "She's got you over a barrel. You are paying an outlandish sum to an administrative assistant because you either like her or you feel guilty about our father. Neither is a good reason." Turning toward his brother, he muttered, "Darn, Oakley. What were you thinking? I thought you were smarter than this."

He was thinking of the kiss and the way her silky hair had felt between his fingers…and how her bottom had fit so perfectly in his hands.

"She's a great admin, and she's not expecting to become Mrs. Fortune," Oakley said. "I want to keep her around. That's all it is."

Evanston scoffed. "You're a fool. How do you know she's not simply waiting for you to do something so she can sue you? Did you ever think she might want revenge, especially since Dad's frivolous suit almost bankrupted her? In fact, when she fired herself, you never should have rehired her."

"She's not going to sue me," Oakley insisted. He couldn't tell them why without bringing up the kiss.

"Now you sound as naive as Cheyenne," his brother grumbled.

"Hey," Cheyenne protested. "Stop being so cynical. I think it's sweet. I've met her—she's nice."

"You should stop being so gullible and trusting," Evanston replied, undaunted.

"You're just distrusting because you're divorced," she pointed out. "Not all women are like your ex, or Oakley's."

"And you wonder why I always say you're Susie Sunshine," Evanston said.

"Hey." Jagger entered the conversation and attempted to diffuse the growing tension. "Oakley's a big boy. You did learn your lesson the first time, right, bro? By marrying? Of course you did. You need to be more like me, embracing the bachelor life. Women are to be sampled and enjoyed, like this fine wine."

"You've enjoyed enough of them," Maisey retorted. "Hence the earlier call for you to grow up now that you're thirty."

"Besides, who doesn't want what our parents had?" Avery asked. "One thing about Dad—he was one hundred percent committed to Mom. And they truly loved each other, madly and deeply. That's what I want."

"Me too," Cheyenne said.

Oakley wanted that as well, and for a second his brain made the leap and he wondered what it would be like to have Rachel as a life mate. They could raise Allie together. Would she want other kids? Rachel was an excellent mother.

"As for your admin—" Evanston's voice snapped Oakley back to attention and that fact that Rachel was absolutely off limits "—maybe next time you simply extend her lunch or allow her to work from home a few days a week. That might be a better option than lavishing her with baby gifts."

"Sure. Good idea," he mumbled.

"And, bro, I have a bunch of women friends I can introduce you to if you're ready to get back out there," Jagger said. "You know, dip your toe in the water without committing."

"I have no desire to have a bunch of one-night stands or meaningless relationships. I thought I'd be happily married and have kids of my own by now. Have that love like our parents." Oakley shrugged. "It didn't work out, and I'm fine. Okay, maybe a little disappointed. But I'm not desperate. Right now I'm cool with being alone, and when the universe thinks it's the right time, the right woman will drop into my lap." Or she'd stumble into him when he was sitting on his desk and he'd crash his mouth to hers—one of the best kisses of his entire life. He didn't dare speak the last part aloud. He had to bury it deep. Rachel had asked him to act professional, and he would. No more desire, no more lustful thoughts. He didn't want to lose her. That would be unthinkable.

"You know, you could devise a few tests to make sure she's loyal to you and that you can trust her." Evanston set his empty wineglass down.

Oakley wished he'd ordered another bottle. "Do tell," he said, knowing his brother planned on doing so whether he wanted him to or not.

"This is what I'd do," Evanston began, getting that look that showed he was deep in thought. "I'd start simple. Leave some family documents on your desk, nothing too sensitive. Not Dad's bills, but something. Or maybe Cheyenne's volunteer schedule. See if it stays confidential or if suddenly everyone in town knows our business."

"Rachel is *not* like that!" Oakley snapped. "She's a good person." He'd seen it with his own eyes, and while he thought he could sit there and hear his brother out, all of this was beginning to tick him off.

Evanston stubbornly pushed on. "Maybe even have someone call the office pretending to be from the media—fishing for information about Dad's latest antics or the family. I mean, we are new to the Fortune family. They could make up a story about us. If she has some sort of revenge agenda, she might confirm it."

Oakley sucked his lips under, silently fuming. That was the last thing Rachel would do. His gut told him he could trust her. Sure, he'd been wrong about his ex, but that was a different story. He'd seen the signs and ignored them, convinced he could fix things. So enamored by the idea of love and marriage, he hadn't considered what type of partner would suit him best. He'd taken the easy route, assuming he'd grow into love and by then they were deep into wedding planning. And like a plane that had to take off no matter what, he'd simply shown up at the altar and prayed it would work out. It hadn't. Instead he and his ex-wife had drifted apart almost from day one.

"Also, stop being so careful about your personal calendar," his brother continued. "Leave it open on your computer when you step out. See if she respects your privacy or starts asking why you're seeing Dr. Morrison twice a week."

"Who is Dr. Morrison?" Avery interjected.

"It's a name I made up," Evanston said. "If she's looking for ammunition against the family, your personal information is a gold mine. Same for something from your past from Dallas that you could let slip."

"These are all ridiculous suggestions," Cheyenne said, rising to Oakley's defense. "She might be good for him."

"You like everyone." When Cheyenne glared at him, Evanston pushed his empty glass forward. "Fine. I'm just saying it's better for Oakley to find out Rachel's true nature before he's in too deep. You might be too naive and gullible at times, Cheyenne, but our brother is far too trusting and nice."

"He *is* a nice guy," Maisey agreed. "Sorry, Oakley, but your sending her all those gifts proves that. It was a kind gesture, but be sure things don't get misconstrued."

"I won't." Oakley was at the end of his patience with this conversation. He liked Rachel and knew her to be none of the things Evanston insinuated. A kiss like that couldn't be faked, and he could see how much she enjoyed her job.

"If you're sure," Maisey said. "We love you and only want what's best for you. You know that."

He shrugged. "Whatever. I really don't want to discuss this anymore. Don't we have anything else to talk about than my nonexistent love life and my admin? How about the dessert we ordered? In fact, our server is coming this way." Grateful for the diversion, he reached for his water glass.

Saved by the crème brûlée.

Chapter Eight

To his credit, and perhaps to her great disappointment, Rachel quickly discovered Oakley was a man of his word. By Tuesday, he hadn't mentioned the kiss, nor did he act as if said liplock had happened. They were strictly business as usual as the days went by.

"Oakley?" She knocked on the door to his office and waited until he looked up. When he did, she ignored the way her heart rate increased. He looked incredibly handsome today. He'd rolled the sleeves of a crisp white dress shirt to his elbows, exposing his muscular forearms, and unfastened the top two buttons at his collar, revealing an expanse of neck and a hint of chest. She swallowed, her knees weakening, when he gave her a friendly smile.

"Hey, how are things going out there?"

She returned his smile. "Good, but I keep getting these calls from someone at a place called the Rodeo Network, but then they hang up. I did an internet search, but there's no website and I can't find a company with that name. There are a few organizations that have that name incorporated in them, but I can't confirm this group exists. It's strange."

Oakley's frown creased his forehead. "Just block the phone number. I'm sure it's just a scam or some sort of phishing. If they find another way to reach you, let me know and I'll take more aggressive action to make it stop."

She nibbled her lower lip. "If you're sure you can do that. The calls came from an anonymous number. Are you sure your rivals aren't trying to get insider information? Because it is weird. Like, what are they trying to find out?"

"I have no idea, but I'm sure it's not corporate espionage."

She could not tell what he was thinking and it worried her. "If you say so, then I won't fret about it any longer. By the way, I also came to tell you I'm about to meet Jenny for lunch."

"Enjoy yourself. I'll be on a conference call with the Dallas VPs. And thanks again for reminding me I'd left out some of my dad's medical papers yesterday. Not sure how I got so forgetful."

"It's not like you to misplace things. Must be the fact that you have the rodeo next weekend." When she'd returned from lunch, she'd found the papers, seen what they were and immediately brought them to him. "Any updates on that?"

"That's what the conference call is for," he reminded her.

"True." She hated the awkwardness that now existed between them. She'd wanted them to be professional, but this felt stilted and perfunctory. "How's Johnny Doe doing? Any new developments?" She hadn't asked about him in a while.

Oakley absently twirled a pen between his thumb and forefingers. "Still no memory. Cheyenne told me he's had a post-operative CT scan to confirm the hematoma evacuation and assess the remaining swelling. She said the scan looked good, and that he hasn't had any seizures. Since it's been about a week, most likely they'll be moving him from the ICU to a neurological ward today or tomorrow. He should get his sutures out soon—or maybe they're staples. I don't remember exactly what she said. But he's stable, and that's a good thing."

"But still no clue why he called out your dad's name?" Rachel found that as odd as Oakley did.

His shrug caused her to shift her focus to his strong, broad shoulders. "None. And I took a DNA test to see if that would help, but it won't come back for several more weeks. They said it might be nearer to the end of September."

She knew that all these unanswered questions had to be frustrating for everyone. "Hopefully, it resolves quickly, and he gets his memory back. As I keep saying, I can't imagine being in the hospital and not knowing who I am."

"I'm going to visit him again soon. With the showcase this upcoming weekend, I've been too busy to get to the hospital lately, but Cheyenne has been checking in and she's keeping me posted."

"Okay. Well, let me know if you learn anything. I'm invested in this mystery now. If you don't need anything else…" When Oakley shook his head, she added, "Then I'm off to lunch. We're trying the new place." She named the restaurant, which was located in the next town over. Everyone had been raving about it, so Rachel was excited to try the food there.

"You'll tell Jenny good things about our working relationship, I hope." For a long moment, Oakley held her gaze.

"I'm telling her only what relates to the business," she reassured him.

Oakley's expression relaxed into relief. "Perfect. And since you have a twenty-minute drive, take all the time you need. If you ever have reason to extend your lunch, feel free. You do more work in one hour than many in my Dallas office. I'll see you when you get back."

"That's kind." It was also unnecessary, but she wouldn't tell him that, on the off chance she ever needed to take Allie to the doctor. The place Jenny had discovered was crowded when Rachel arrived, but Rachel found her friend easily. Jenny gave her a hug before they took their seats.

"You look happier than I've ever seen you," Jenny observed.

"Really?" Rachel reached for the sweet tea Jenny had preordered for her. "I guess I am. Things are finally feeling settled, not that I trust them."

How could she, when despite Oakley ignoring their kiss like she asked him to, she still felt its impact? Even thinking about their steamy embrace had the power to send desire rushing through her. Luckily, she was sitting down, so she could dip her head and Jenny couldn't see the heat spreading across her cheeks.

"The shoe won't necessarily drop," Jenny promised as she reached for her own glass. "You know I follow up with all my clients, and so Oakley and I had a long video chat yesterday afternoon."

Rachel coughed as some tea went down wrong. "I didn't know when that was happening." She knew her boss would give Jenny a performance review, but she hadn't expected one so soon.

"And now it has. You've been working for him for two weeks. Believe me, you have nothing to worry about. He's singing your praises. He called you one of the best admins he's ever had, including saying you're better than the one who retired, and he adored her. You've certainly made an impact on him."

He'd also made an impact on her. If she wasn't focusing on Allie or work, she was remembering how his lips had felt on hers, and how cherished she'd felt being in his arms. She had to put things into perspective. "He feels bad for me since his dad sued me and caused me to almost go bankrupt."

Jenny's eyebrows formed a skeptical line. "Perhaps, but he wouldn't keep you on if you didn't do the work," she pointed out practically. She opened her menu. "You're good at what you do, Rachel. Don't sell yourself short. Now, what are you thinking of ordering?"

Rachel studied the menu and decided on the lunch-size barbecue chicken salad. Jenny chose a honey barbecue chicken wrap and fries. "So tell me what else is new?" Jenny asked. "How are your parents doing?"

Grateful for the switch in topics, she and her bestie spent the next hour eating and chatting. Jenny told her how seeing Allie made her want to have another baby, but how her husband wasn't ready. "We didn't have an easy time conceiving last time, so I don't want to wait."

"Despite my ex, I'm glad I have Allie." Rachel leaned back as the server removed her empty bowl. "I'd like her to have siblings, this time hopefully with the right partner, if that ever happens. I've sworn off men, remember?"

Jenny made sympathetic noises. "Does Allie have cousins? You're not that close to your siblings, are you?"

"Not like Oakley is with his. They're all moving to Emerald Ridge so they can be together—they're *that* close. I've never experienced anything like it. My siblings and I don't even exchange birthday cards. A rare text if that." Rachel felt her cheeks heat. The last person she'd wanted to bring back into the conversation was her sexy boss, especially as Jenny's eyebrow had lifted.

"Now you have me curious," her friend said.

"They are always doing things together, like lunches and dinners. They'll video-call each other at least once a week as well. I see my siblings on major holidays—that is, if I'm lucky. The Fortunes' father might be a crass, horrid man, but it's clear that they love him and each other. It's a bit enviable, not that I'm softening toward Clemons." She gave an involuntary shudder. "He's a menace. I can't believe he refused to pay for a haircut. Look how good of a job Sofia did. Honestly, I still can't wrap my brain around the idea that Oakley's related to him. They are nothing alike."

"As long as you don't fall for Oakley like his previous admin, all will be well," Jenny warned. "Eyes on the prize. You have about thirty days until you're off probation and get the company benefits that come with that."

"Believe me, I won't forget. I'd be a fool to throw this job away now that we have the issues with Clemons resolved and Oakley said his father won't be bothering me. It's hard for me to trust, but I'm hoping for the best."

Jenny nodded. "From what you've told me, Oakley doesn't trust easily either, not personally or professionally. So if he tells me you're working out great, you must be doing something right. Whatever it is, keep doing it."

"I plan on it." Minus kissing him again, of course. She checked the movement of her hand before she touched her lips. Bad enough she had to keep remembering not to touch her hair once she styled it. Now she couldn't rub her lips, lest she give away her nerves.

When lunch ended, Jenny insisted on paying the bill, saying it was a business expense, and she and Rachel hugged goodbye in the parking lot. Since her friend had another appointment at a business near the café, they drove in opposite directions.

Rachel was five minutes from the outskirts of Emerald Ridge when she heard a sudden pop followed by what sounded like a hiss. Steam began seeping out from under the hood, and a frantic glance at her dash showed the temperature gauge needle rising rapidly into the red zone. She gripped the steering wheel tighter as the car lost power. Thankfully she was on a two-lane highway and made it to the gravel shoulder as the engine began to knock and ping. She put on her hazard lights, turned off the engine and called Oakley. He answered immediately. "Hey, I'm going to be needing that extended lunch after all. Something happened to my radiator, and it overheated. I've pulled over."

"Where are you?" Oakley asked.

She told him.

"I know where that's at. Lock the doors and stay in the car. I'm on my way." Before she could answer, he'd hung up.

As the car interior was already beginning to heat, Rachel cracked the windows. Several cars whizzed past but didn't stop. Soon one went past, made a U-turn and pulled up behind her, and parked with hazards flashing. Through her driver's side window, Rachel felt a wave of relief as she saw Oakley approach. While she could have handled this crisis, it was wonderful to have a knight in shining armor coming to her rescue. Oakley came to the passenger side, and she unlocked the car. He opened the door and leaned inside. She was never so grateful to see him. "Are you okay?"

"Shaken, but otherwise fine. This was not on my bucket list for the day." Or in her budget.

"Pop the hood and let me take a look."

Rachel reached under the dashboard and found the latch. The hood unlocked with a loud click. As Oakley lifted the hood and secured it, more steam escaped. She glanced out the rearview mirror, and seeing no cars coming, safely climbed out and met him at the front of her car. The sweet smell of coolant hit her nose, and she drew back. "Can we fix it?"

"Sadly, no. You're going to need a tow truck. See that?" He pointed to a hose dangling loose. Below it, a puddle of coolant spread across the ground. "That's your radiator hose…everything's leaked out. Looks like the rubber cracked and broke. Probably was rotting from the inside out. It happens."

"I should have known." This was one reason why cars needed routine maintenance.

"I'm doubtful you could have known. Unless you're a mechanic, everything would have probably looked fine. The hose failed from inside out because of the internal pressures and temperatures created when driving. It is an older car."

An eleven-year-old car she'd been putting off getting serviced since she hadn't had a good enough job or enough money.

"We should get you a new one," Oakley said. He must have sensed her panic for he began to close the hood. It landed with a loud, reverberating clang. "That's a project for another day. For now, let's call a tow truck. I'll get your stuff swapped out and moved into my SUV. If you need a car, you can borrow mine until we get you a rental." He dialed a number, issued some rapid-fire orders. "Come on, let's grab your stuff. My car has air conditioning and it's hot out."

Rachel had to admit waiting in Oakley's luxury vehicle was far better than sitting in hers. The leather seats were not only comfortable, but they came complete with cooling fans. Those complemented the powerful air conditioning, one that worked far better than hers ever had. She actually shivered. Oakley noticed and adjusted the temperature. The ferocity of the air exiting the vents lessened.

"How was your lunch?" he asked.

"Good, until the drive home." She sighed. "I knew better than to keep delaying getting my car to the shop. What's that saying? An ounce of prevention is worth a pound of cure? I'm praying that didn't blow the engine. I have to get this running. A new car is not yet in the budget. Neither was this repair. I'm sure it'll be pricey."

"We'll have them look at it and see what they can do. Let me have your key." A tow truck came into view, made a U-turn and backed itself up to Rachel's car. Her key in hand, Oakley went to greet the driver. Within minutes, he was back. "They'll call you once they know what's wrong, beyond the obvious of course, and give you an estimate."

She secured her seat belt and leaned her head back as Oakley pulled around her parked car. "Thanks for getting me and for telling Jenny I was a good employee."

"Actually, I said you're great. But you might not feel I'm a great boss when you hear what I need to ask of you next."

"No late hours tonight, please. I'm stressed enough." And now she was more stressed. What did he need to ask her? And she hoped he didn't want to discuss that kiss, especially as she couldn't put it out of her mind. It lurked there, just under the surface, an ever permanent reminder of how easy it would be to cross a line if she wasn't careful.

He grinned. "Nope. Not tonight. Not adding anything to your stress today." He turned his attention back to the road. "However, as you know, our signature rodeo event, the showcase, is this weekend in Dallas. I'm leaving early Thursday morning and won't be back until sometime Tuesday afternoon and…"

They'd reached town and he made a turn onto Emerald Ridge Boulevard. "And…?" Rachel prompted as he'd dropped the thread.

"I'd like you to go to Dallas with me for the weekend, or at least Thursday and Friday."

"What?"

Her shock must have been evident because he backtracked quickly. "For work reasons, of course. It's the showcase, and your accompanying me would give you an opportunity to meet your Dallas counterparts. You know everything inside and out. It would be great for you to be on-site rather than via video. The company will, of course, pay for overtime and for your hotel and meals." His fingers tapped against the steering wheel as they waited at a stoplight. "I'll understand if you don't want to leave Allie. You could make the drive instead if you'd rather."

"Not without a car."

"I said you can borrow mine. Or we can rent you something."

Again Oakley showed how bighearted he could be, but logistically it was still a nightmare. With traffic and the distance she'd need to travel, she'd be on the road far more than she wanted to be.

"Tell you what. Let me see if Taylor is willing to babysit. I'm sure I could be in Dallas at least Thursday night and then return to Emerald Ridge on Friday evening." The overtime she'd make might be enough to pay for the repairs.

"Great. Let me know tomorrow." He parked the car and they walked toward the office. "I have a few things to wrap up and then I'm going to drop by the hospital before I meet my siblings. We're doing dinner earlier this week since I'll be heading to Dallas." He unlocked the door to the office and stepped back so she could enter first. "Home sweet office."

He left her then, and Rachel settled back into the tasks that had doubled in the short time she'd been sitting on the roadside. She'd let Jenny know about her car, and that she was good as she could walk to work. She didn't have any appointments scheduled for the remainder of the week, and she could always have groceries delivered this once. She would find a way to survive without borrowing Oakley's SUV. Although, it was sweet and generous of him to make the offer, and to have dropped everything to come and get her.

As for his asking her to go to Dallas? She hadn't been back since she'd moved, and she hadn't been away from Allie overnight since her daughter was born. It might be nice to have a getaway and meet everyone at the main office, but at the same time, Oakley was pure temptation. Spending more time with him might be dangerous. She could not let one kiss make her believe that there was anything more.

He stopped by her desk and chatted before he left the office. She stayed for another hour before heading home, where she found Taylor in the kitchen with Allie. When her daughter saw her, she grinned.

"You have a mouth full of banana," Rachel said. She leaned and kissed Allie on the forehead, moving aside before her daughter's sticky fingers managed to find their way into Rachel's loose hair. "How was she today?"

Taylor handed Rachel a glass of water. "She's the easiest baby. Seriously, she makes it fun. I could watch her forever." She made silly faces at Allie, who clapped. Bits of banana splattered.

"Would you be willing to watch her overnight?" Rachel asked. "Say this Thursday? Or is that your book club night?"

"No, it's next Thursday. And where are you going?"

"Dallas." Rachel explained the situation while using a wet washcloth to clean Allie's fingers.

"Do you think this is wise? I have no issues watching Allie, but it's an away trip with your boss. He already has been in your home."

"It's nothing." She would not tell Taylor about the kiss. "I'll be with everyone else from the office as well."

"If that's the case, then maybe you should stay the weekend and take some time for yourself. It's a rodeo. You also have friends there. Visit them. I'll bring Allie with me to my family's picnic and she can hang out with the other kids."

Rachel's lip quivered. Now that the reality of attending was possible, she didn't know if she wanted to leave. "I've never been away from her."

Taylor's no-nonsense smile was still warm, encouraging and sympathetic. "All the more reason to give yourself a break. You need some 'me' time, Rachel. While Allie is important, so are you. You cannot let her become your entire life to the point where you lose yourself."

"I know but…"

"No buts. One day she'll walk out of here to go to college or she'll move across the country and where will you be then?"

Rachel didn't even want to think that far ahead.

"It goes faster than you know it," Taylor warned. "You're allowed to be a mother and also have your own life and interests. Doing so doesn't make you any less of a mom."

"It will be good for my career to meet the other staff.

When he moves the entire company here, I'll know them already. And I don't want to be an admin my entire life."

"Exactly. Perhaps you can be a vice president someday or something. Don't sell yourself short or miss something because you were afraid to take a risk. Just be smart about things and keep yourself professional at all times."

"Believe me, I learned that lesson with Allie's baby daddy."

"Ga!" Allie said, which came across a lot like a warped version of "go."

The thought overwhelmed, but it wasn't something she should turn down. "Okay, I'll take the weekend. It might be nice to connect with some of my other friends, too." Rachel hadn't really kept up with any, not because of their lack of trying, but mostly because she'd been so busy juggling everything that she'd not had the minutes to spare.

The older woman gave a satisfied nod. "Good. That's what I like to hear. And when you get back Monday, I can't wait for you to tell me everything that happened. I love the rodeo, and you'll have VIP access. If you meet Cody Fallsworth, can you get me his autograph?"

Cody Fallsworth was a rodeo champion and a huge celebrity. "He is going to be there. If I can, I will get it. Promise."

"Fingers crossed," Taylor said, brushing her hand over her flushed cheeks. "That'll make my day. I'm almost jealous—I'd love to be in the same room with that man. You're going to have a great time."

"It's work."

"It'll also be *fun*," her neighbor argued.

"You're right—it will be," Rachel agreed. She reached for her phone. While she was still unsure about leaving Allie and nervous about the implications of being in Dallas with Oakley, Taylor was right. She did need to have her own life. She texted Oakley before she changed her mind: I have a sitter for the entire weekend.

Dallas, here I come.

Oakley was walking into the restaurant when he received Rachel's message. "What's that goofy grin about?" Jagger asked as Oakley approached the table.

"Nothing. Just good news about the rodeo." Oakley liked Rachel's message and shoved his phone into his pocket. His siblings had already arrived at Captain's for their weekly dinner, but there was no sign of his father. "A lot's riding on this weekend."

"I see what you did there." Cheyenne giggled. "You're funny."

Oakley gave a shake of his head. "That's me. So punny." He reached for his water goblet. "Sorry I'm late, but I got caught up at the hospital. I went by to check on our friend Johnny Doe." The server came by and Oakley ordered an old-fashioned.

"What's the latest?" Maisey asked.

"They did a speech and memory assessment, and his speech is intact but with word-finding difficulties. His EEGs have been good and he hasn't had any seizures. But he still has the severe retrograde amnesia. They've moved him to the neuro ward and have started him on some speech therapy. He's been assigned a social worker. She told me the sutures will be out before the weekend."

"That's good news at least," Evanston said.

"But we still don't have the DNA back," Oakley reminded him. "Or know who's in the picture."

Evanston reached for his cocktail. "Speaking of that baby picture, Cheyenne sent me the picture you took of it, so I did a reverse search on the internet. Unfortunately, I came up empty."

"Worth a try, though," Avery said.

"Exactly," Evanston murmured before he took a sip. As he lowered his glass, he glanced at his watch. "Where's Dad? He should have been here long before now."

"Do you think he had an accident?" Cheyenne asked, her forehead creasing in worry.

"I'm sure he's simply running late like I was," Oakley soothed. "You know he's been late before." Although it was rare.

"Maybe he forgot that this was an entire family dinner," Maisey said. "We do seem to get together a lot, just us kids."

"I'm texting him." Cheyenne reached for her phone, but before she'd swiped it open, they heard a commotion coming from the hostess stand.

"I said I can see them and know where I'm going." Clemons's voice carried as he made his way toward the table.

"I wonder what has him in knots now?" Maisey asked.

"He's clearly agitated about something," Evanston agreed. "You can see it from here."

"Let's hope it's nothing major this time," Avery added. "I'm tired of the drama."

When their dad arrived at the table, he didn't even sit but wrapped his fingers around the back of the empty chair instead. "Mewington's gone," he announced.

Everyone gasped.

"Oh no! Your poor cat." Cheyenne was already on her feet, and she rounded the table toward her dad. "What happened? This is so tragic and unexpected. I'm so sorry. How did he die?"

Clemons brushed off her attempt to give him a hug. "Did you hear me say he's dead?" he snapped. "He's *not* dead. He's gone. Someone opened the catio door, and he's vanished. Escaped. I've been calling him all day. I can't find him anywhere. I swear, if someone took him and I find them, I'm suing them or putting them in prison."

"Dad, it'll be okay." This time Clemons let Cheyenne hug him as she'd started crying.

"We'll find him," Avery said, standing. Like Oakley, she'd noticed her dad appeared shaken.

He was already on the internet searching for what to do for a lost cat. "I found some advice online. One thing is to put Mewington's litter box and some of your worn clothes outside as that could help him come home. Have you begun searching? Says here that cats who get out usually hide close by rather than wander far."

"Someone took him, I know it," Clemons choked out. "He's a valuable cat. I looked everywhere and called him. Someone stole him!"

"We don't know that," Oakley said. "We should look under porches and in garages, and as it's almost dusk, this is a great time to go find him."

"We should post on social media," Avery said. "I can do that."

"And make flyers and hang them," Maisey added. "I'll help with that."

"He's long gone," Clemons insisted, his chin quivering. "You know the haters in this town can't stand me. They hate that I'm a Fortune. Hate that I'm not going to put up with their bad attitudes. I wouldn't put it past them for one of them to have let him out on purpose!"

Oakley didn't want to upset his dad further by suggesting that perhaps the cat simply figured out a way to open the door and escape all on his own. Mewington was quite the genius. They'd found him hiding in a closet once. Then there had been the time he'd been spotted inside a dresser drawer. Each time the cat had been quite proud of giving them a scare. Probably this disappearance would be similar and they'd find the cat quickly. "Let's focus on getting Mewington back safely. The website I was on says that most indoor cats are recovered within a three-house radius, so it's not time to panic."

Unless someone had stolen Mewington because he was a pure-blooded Maine coon. Despite his dad's assertions, Oakley didn't want to entertain that thought.

"We'll get him back, Dad," Maisey reassured. "Let's go look for him now."

When the server handed Oakley his drink, he asked for the bill for the table. He'd go through one of those late-night drive-throughs and get something to eat once they found the beloved purebred cat. He took a few sips before setting the rest on the table. "I got the check," he told his siblings. "Go with Dad and I'll meet you there and we can search."

But hours later, there was still no sign of the kitty. They'd searched everywhere, shining flashlights under cars and into bushes. Clemons left the door to the catio open, and he set out food. Meanwhile, Jagger set up cameras that would alert their father if triggered by a cat-sized creature.

It was almost 2:00 a.m. before they called it quits. By then Avery had posted Mewington on all the lost pet and neighborhood apps.

"I'll laminate these flyers tomorrow and we can start hanging them," Maisey said. "Hopefully he'll be in his catio when you wake up tomorrow morning."

As he trundled off to bed, Clemons was still grumbling about how someone had to have opened the catio door.

"We have to find that cat," Evanston said as he locked the door to the house behind them. The siblings paused at the end of the sidewalk near their respective cars.

"I'll come over first thing tomorrow morning," Avery promised. "I can make the time. That way someone is here when Dad wakes up."

Oakley nodded. "Thank you. I can help tomorrow, but I've got to be in Dallas on Thursday and won't be back until late Tuesday."

"No, we've got this," Jagger said. "We know how important this weekend is for your business. There's enough of us to help Dad. We'll text you if we find Mewington."

"Then I'll be at the office if you need me," Oakley said.

On a routine patrol, a police car drove down the street. The officer stopped, but Oakley didn't recognize him. As Evanston began to tell the officer who they were and about the lost cat, Oakley checked under his car. He then waved at his siblings as he drove off. Before turning on the radio, he said a prayer that they'd find Mewington quickly, then threw the manifestation out into the universe.

His father was still grieving the loss of his wife, not to mention already being on edge from the move to Emerald Ridge. Fate wouldn't be so cruel as to let their dad lose his precious cat as well.

Oakley was tired and hungry. He gave a huge yawn and glanced at the dashboard clock. None of the drive-through places were open this late. If he worked from home tomorrow, he could get a few hours of sleep and be available should his dad or siblings need him. He dictated a text to Rachel before turning off the car and shutting the garage door. Then, he strolled into the house and rummaged through the mostly empty refrigerator. Peanut butter and jelly would have to do.

It was probably for the best he didn't see Rachel tomorrow anyway. His heart had jumped when she'd confirmed she'd go to Dallas. He was excited about everything there was to show her, from the actual rodeo to the people in the office he wanted her to meet. He planned to ensure she had one of the best seats in the house, especially as she'd said she loved attending rodeos with her dad. After all her hard work these past few weeks with organizing and coordinating, she deserved to fully enjoy the weekend.

But her going to Dallas with him also meant they'd be in tight confines, from the car ride there and back to attending meetings and the Sunday night banquet, alongside rodeo participants and his employees. That wasn't even including the opening events, such as the cocktail party.

Rapid fire thoughts raced around his head as Oakley slathered the peanut butter onto white sandwich bread. Despite the fact the sun would be up in a few hours, he found himself wide awake. This was shaping up to be a great weekend.

He simply had to remember to be professional and that Rachel being there didn't mean it was a date.

But as he finally climbed into his bed, he had to admit knowing he'd have an entire weekend with her made it feel like one.

And he didn't mind one bit.

Chapter Nine

Thursday morning, Rachel couldn't quite calm the butterflies flitting about her stomach. While she was traveling to Dallas, her former home city, and not somewhere exciting like Hawaii or Australia, it was her first hotel trip in over two years. The last one had been with the ex, and she'd mostly found herself ignored unless he wanted sex. This trip was with Oakley, meaning it promised to be far different.

First, working with the Dallas event staff, she'd made the hotel reservations. Because of his schedule and position as owner of the company, Oakley had a penthouse suite with an attached twelve-person conference room. Those VPs staying on-site were in junior suites. She'd reserved a regular room for herself. Because the hotel was the location for many of the offsite events, the hotel was fully booked with those either attending the rodeo showcase or participating in it. She wasn't expecting an upgrade, nor did she need one.

She'd packed carefully, including several nice cocktail dresses, and her medium-sized suitcase sat next to her desk along with her computer tote. She'd helped set the agenda for the entire weekend, including her and Oakley's parts in it. For the Sunday evening award ceremony, she figured one of her simple black sheaths would be perfect. Besides, it was the one that still fit and hadn't faded. Friday and Saturday night were competition nights, both professional and amateur level. In addition to the competition rounds, a variety of vendors would be selling everything from souvenirs to T-shirts to a wide variety of foods.

Rachel glanced at the corner of her computer. She'd scheduled them to leave by nine-fifteen, so she rose to go make another pot of coffee that they could put into insulated bottles and take on the road. She had the pot brewing in the kitchen when she heard the door to the office open. "I'll be right out," she called. She wiped her hands on a paper towel and stepped out into the room.

And froze. Clemons Frost…no Clemons *Fortune* now… stood there wearing a white linen suit similar to the one he'd worn the day Allie had projectile vomited.

"You!" they both said at the same time.

Rachel recovered first. She calmed her nerves by striding to the trash and tossing the paper towel. "Mr. Fortune. I'll let your son know you're here since he's not expecting you." In fact, she thought Oakley had told his father not to come to the office in order to keep it a safe space for her. If he had, Clemons had violated that directive.

"Dad?" Oakley came to the doorway. "What are you doing here?"

"What is *she* doing here?" Clemons asked instead.

"She works here as my administrative assistant. I told you this, and that because of you, I had to hire her back after she quit. I also told you never to come by the office without calling me first."

Clemons glared at his son. "You should have gotten rid of her. She's trouble. Her baby ruined my suit. What the hell were you thinking? Then you always were a fool for a pretty face."

Rachel bit back her immediate retort of "How dare you." She tucked her lips under and mentally began to count to ten. She refused to let Clemons get to her or to be unprofessional.

She didn't get far before Oakley gritted out, "Dad, she's standing right here so you will *not* speak about her like that. She's my administrative assistant, and she's excellent at her job."

"You're too soft, boy. You're blind to the truth." Clemons launched the blow with extreme vehemence. "She's probably already trying to get her claws in you. Speaking of claws..." His eyes narrowed. "You snuck into my house and let my cat out, didn't you?"

"Dad!" Oakley's rebuke was clear.

Rachel couldn't hold her silence. "I don't even know what you're talking about."

Clemons snarled his disbelief. "My beloved cat is gone. The catio door was open. You did it—I know it. You wanted retribution for me suing you earlier in the year. It's not enough that you are trying to get your hooks into my son—you went after my cat so you could get to me directly."

"I did nothing of the sort." She took a deep breath as she'd begun shaking from the vitriol Clemons had launched.

"Ha. Good try. I'm sure you did. You have access to where I live. That's why you work for my son, to get back at me. It's part of your scheme."

Rachel closed a mouth that had dropped open in full disbelief. Her mother had always maintained that if you didn't have anything nice to say, then it was best to say nothing at all, and currently the curse words ready to spring forth were probably not entirely professional. And she didn't want Oakley to see her like that, even if Clemons deserved a good berating. The man was insufferable. How *dare* he?

Oakley had moved to stand next to Clemons, as if ready to block any movement of his father toward Rachel. "Dad, Rachel had nothing to do with Mewington going missing. I know he didn't come home yet, but we will find him. The reward posters are going up as we speak. Right now, you need to apologize to Rachel, and then you need to go meet my sisters. They're planning on helping you."

"It's your help I want, and for you to open your eyes and see the traitor in your midst," Clemons snapped, his cheeks puffing.

"Dad." Oakley spoke calmly, as if he'd been through this with his father many times before. "If you won't apologize, that's fine, but I will not have you insulting Rachel in my office or returning if you can't be civil. Now, you need to go, and so do I as I have meetings in Dallas and have to be there by noon."

His father's glare never wavered until he suddenly noticed Rachel's suitcase. As the hard-sided case was lavender colored, it was clearly not Oakley's. "She's going with you?" His face reddened as he enunciated each word. "Boy, I hoped I hadn't raised no fool, but you don't know her like I do. I see what you can't, that she's probably like your previous admin, who—let me remind you—was a gold digger. She's the same. An opportunist." Clemons threw out the accusation with immense satisfaction and complete smugness that he was 100 percent correct in his assessment.

Rachel hadn't known Oakley long, but she'd never seen

his face blanch with pure indignant mortification before. His arms tightened at his sides, as if he were resisting the urge to raise them. Rachel understood. She felt the same. She wanted to reach out and throttle Clemons, perhaps shake some sense into him.

"Dad, now you owe me an apology," Oakley said. His father's eyes widened at Oakley's words, especially as they'd been delivered in a tone that indicated Oakley's patience with his father's unsubstantiated accusations and abhorrent behaviors had run out. Or, in other words, Clemons had exceeded Oakley's daily tolerance limit.

"I owe no one nothin'," Clemons retorted, but he did appear more subdued, as if recognizing he'd crossed a line.

"Yes, you do. Rachel is one of the kindest, gentlest people I've ever met. As for her daughter, she's a precious gem and the sweetest baby ever. Allie is adorable, which you would have realized had you not thrown a tantrum when she got sick and threw up. Instead of being understanding, you were abhorrent and went overboard. Your behavior was as unacceptable then as it is now. You did yourself no favors in the eyes of the public, and right now, if you weren't my father, you and I wouldn't be having this conversation."

Oakley drew a breath. "Rachel is a great admin, one of the best I've had, including the one who didn't want to relocate from Dallas. She's smart and well-respected, and you'd do well to remember that this is my life and that I'm wise enough to know who to let into it and who to keep out."

"You didn't—"

Oakley cut him off. "You can keep your thoughts to yourself regarding my failed marriage and my business acumen. I'm no boy. I'm a grown man, and if I want your opinion, I will ask you. Otherwise, stop insulting me and my admin." He cleared his throat, leveling his father with another stern look. "While I am used to your attitude, that doesn't mean it is acceptable or allowed, especially in my office. And Rachel has already experienced enough of your bad behavior, so I will not let you continue to insult her now. It's wrong, and you know it."

Clemons's eyes widened. His face had turned a deep purple. About to say something, he clamped his mouth shut, turned and stormed out the door, leaving it wide open. Oakley stepped halfway out into the hall. Then he pulled the door shut and tossed the dead bolt. "I apologize. He shouldn't have spoken to you like that."

"He's your father..."

The shake of Oakley's head came fast and furious. "No. There is no excuse for that behavior from anyone, my father or not. His belligerence, unfounded accusations and tirades are childish and not suiting to a man of his age or stature. While I know he's still grieving the loss of my mom, he doesn't get to take it out on those around him. She'd be appalled if she heard him speak that way." He sighed wearily. "I'll be discussing this with my siblings as soon as I return from Dallas. I have half a mind to text them right now, but I don't want to deal with him anymore today lest it spoil our weekend. I'm just truly sorry you had to be subjected to that, today or any day. Never again. Not on my watch."

Her heart swelled. Oakley's words and actions were conclusive proof that he was the type of guy who stood up for what was right and decent. "Thank you."

"And thank *you* for not saying it's okay, because it's not." He ran an agitated hand through his hair, indicating how much the situation had upset him. "Even though

I don't have the right to ask for it, I'd appreciate your discretion."

Her clasped hands opened as if flicking something away. "I'm still angry, but not at you. You've been nothing but kind and generous, and I won't do anything to jeopardize your business or you. You can count on me. You don't deserve what happened either, Oakley. We don't get to pick our parents."

"We do not." His chest heaved, and she felt sorry for him. She had wonderful, loving parents. What must it be like to be the son of Clemons Fortune, walking nightmare?

"Did he really lose his cat?" she asked softly.

Oakley's shoulders sagged with the weight of the world. "Sadly, yes. That's why I was out of the office yesterday. We were up most of the night looking for Mewington. My dad loves that cat. My siblings and I got it for him. He's purebred, but he was at the local shelter. For my dad and Mewington, it was love at first sight."

Rachel knew shelters were often filled with purebred animals. "I'm sorry he lost his cat. That would be horrible for anyone."

Oakley straightened. "True. But I'm still not letting him talk to you like that. Shall we get going? I just have to grab my laptop."

"Of course. I need to do the same." While Oakley retrieved his things, Rachel packed her own computer and went to the kitchen to fill the insulated bottles and clean the coffee pot. She had her computer bag on her shoulder and her fingers wrapped around her suitcase handle when he returned. With her free hand, she held one of the insulated bottles containing the coffee.

"Thanks. And I've got that." He grabbed the handle

and rolled her suitcase. Soon they were in his SUV and on the way to Dallas.

"Doing okay?" he asked her after the first ten miles.

"Yeah. Even though I haven't been living in Emerald Ridge that long, it feels weird to be driving in this direction. Like it's a place from my past. It's sort of bittersweet. I thought about seeing some old friends, but no one is free on short notice, and the schedule's busy, anyway."

"I know exactly how that feels. It's weird to think you've moved on." Oakley got into the passing lane to work around a semitruck. "Does Allie's dad still live in Dallas?"

"He was in Fort Worth, and no. He moved somewhere out of state. Hit the road so he wouldn't have to pay child support. The lawyer I hired couldn't find him."

"Not even through his job? Or his social security number?" Oakley was aghast.

"Not even through that," Rachel admitted. "Maybe he left the country. He'd always talked about living on a beach in Mexico. I could have hired a private investigator to track him down but…"

"Those cost money," Oakley finished.

"Exactly. It's still a sore spot. I thought we were building something special but instead I was simply a buddy to have when we went on trips or to sleep with when he returned. Looking back, it was sex and nothing more." Her cheeks heated. "I can't believe I told you that."

"I don't have the greatest track record with relationships either." He eased back into the right lane. "I was the one confused by what I thought was love. I thought we were building something, but in hindsight, it was all a lie. She wanted what I represented, not who I was."

"How so?"

"Oakley Frost was building his rodeo empire. That was an exciting world to be in except for the long hours it takes to get a company off the ground. While this weekend is all fun and games for those attending, you saw the work it takes to arrange. To get to this level took a lot of blood, sweat and tears."

"Yeah, it *was* a lot of work, and this is your signature event, so everyone but me has been through it several times before. Anything worth doing is worth doing well."

"Exactly my philosophy. And when you reach the top, you have to work to stay there. Building a company is hard, and when it came down to it, I think my ex-wife felt left out, so she found someone else."

"That's a shame," Rachel murmured.

"What, that she decided to pick someone better?"

"No, that you think that's the reason. Not to sound forward, but you're a great guy. You're handsome and kind. Generous to a fault. You're a real catch." Her voice caught on that last word. If he heard it, he ignored it.

"Then how do you explain the cheating? Her deciding monogamy wasn't for her? That there had to be something wrong with me. Was I too selfish? Too cold? She said I didn't prioritize her. Maybe I didn't."

"I can't explain why she cheated or whatever reason made her do what she did. It's not a decision I would ever make. But instead of assuming it's all your fault, perhaps recognize the fact that there was something broken about her. That she needed the thrill of the chase, or the illicitness of it, same as some people crave being high or needing another drink." Rachel slanted a look at him, her tone gentle as she said, "I don't know her, but I do know you shouldn't blame yourself. It took me nine months to figure that out about Mitch. He made his choices. She made hers. The trouble is that we got caught in their inconsiderate cross fire."

"True. That's a great perspective. Thank you. My siblings have said it, but hearing it from you helps. It means something coming from someone who hasn't known me my whole life."

Rachel's confidence grew. "Their actions weren't necessarily designed to make us feel less about ourselves, but that's the impact they had. Their actions were rooted in their own issues, their own narcissism perhaps. What we have to do is shake that off. We don't have to live with the damage they've done—we can move on." She released a sigh. "That's what I'm trying to do. I get knocked down and I get back up. Over and over if that's what it takes."

She turned her head to read one of the giant billboards advertising a fast-food chain. Then she shifted back toward him and gave a curt laugh. "Can you tell my mom's a therapist?"

"She's clearly a good one," Oakley complimented. "That speech made more sense to me than any of the stuff I heard from the guy I paid an exorbitant amount to help me through it."

"She's my biggest cheerleader, aside from Jenny, of course. They help me remember that I'm the one who controls my destiny, and that my past can remain firmly in my past. On the plus side, because of Mitch's defection, I don't have to deal with the nightmare of shared custody. Allie is mine."

"There is that positive." They'd reached the outer suburbs surrounding Dallas, and as the traffic thickened, their conversation turned to easier, less fraught topics. She was laughing at something he'd said—a story from a high school spirit week where he'd ended up covered in gold glitter—when he drove under the hotel portico.

However, she wasn't laughing minutes later after the front desk clerk said she didn't have a room. "How can that be?" Rachel set a reservation printout on the desk. "I have the confirmation right here for this very hotel."

The clerk made rapid keystrokes. "I honestly don't know. We have the rest of the Fortune Rodeo Corporation hotel rooms but somehow this one was cancelled. Perhaps someone extended their stay and that overrode the system. It's a huge error. This shouldn't have happened, but we're full, so we'll need to find you something at one of our nearby sister hotels."

"You don't have an upgrade available?" Oakley leaned his elbow on the counter and peered over.

"No. Because of the rodeo showcase, we're completely full. Every last room is booked." She inserted his keycards into the magnetizer. "I do have your suite ready, Mr. Fortune. I'll call one of the other hotels and see what they can do for Miss Evers. We will upgrade her there, of course, because of the inconvenience."

"That's not acceptable." Oakley pushed the keycard back toward the front desk clerk. "She's not staying at an offsite hotel when the events are happening in this hotel. Give her the bedroom in the penthouse suite. Put it on a separate key. I'll take the couch in the living area."

"Oakley, it's fine," Rachel protested. She didn't want to cause a scene or put him out. Most likely some other VIP had pulled rank. "I can go down the street."

"No, you won't. Change it, please," he said to the hotel employee.

"If you're sure." The clerk glanced between them.

"I'm certain," Oakley insisted. "And be sure to have

your manager call me once I get to the room. I want to speak with them."

"Will do." Relieved, she handed each of them a key. She pointed to Rachel's left. "The express elevators to the penthouse level are down that hall, behind the wall. The porter has your luggage."

"I'm sorry," Rachel said once she and Oakley were alone in the elevator. "You shouldn't have done that. No need for you to give up your room."

"Why not? The sofa bed will be comfortable, and it's not your fault they messed up the reservation. Some manager probably had an irate VIP customer and gave them your room thinking you wouldn't come." A muscle ticked in his jaw. "Hotels shouldn't do that, but believe me, once I speak with them, they'll understand it was the wrong thing to do. And no worries, I'll do it using far less force than my dad would." Oakley pointed to the room number. "This is it. My door's down here."

Rachel pressed the plastic key to her room against the sensor, and the lights turned green. Larger than an average hotel room, the space held a huge king-size bed. In addition to traditional hotel furniture such as a dresser and desk, it had a seating area with love seat and two chairs. She peered through the open doorway into the living area. It had a full dining table, a kitchen, one sofa, two love seats and several armchairs. There was also a huge work desk with a leather chair. The opposite wall contained a door leading to the small conference room.

"I'm going to shut and lock the connecting door and ask you to do the same," she called into the suite. "I don't want anyone to think that we're sharing a space. Your father has already accused me of being a gold digger. I don't need my coworkers to think it, too, or that there's anything untoward between us, especially after your last admin's actions."

He came to the inner doorway. Her breath caught. He was so close. "If that's what you want. Especially after..." He didn't finish the thought and she knew he meant the kiss. "But I'm not going to lock my side. That way you don't need to go out through the hallway."

"But I will. I don't want to catch you doing, well, whatever."

He grinned. "So just knock and wait for me to respond first. Or if it's open, you'll know it's fine to come through and it's just me in here. Although, aside from when I have people in the conference room, it should always be just me in here."

"You never know," Rachel tried to tease, but it fell flat.

"Oh, I know," Oakley stressed with a serious nod. "Believe me, there's no one who tempts me. Well, there is, but we have to remain professional. She can, however, help me ward off the true gold diggers who try to get my attention this weekend."

As a delighted quiver raced through her, Rachel refused to assume that he meant her, even though she was 100 percent positive he did. Confirmation was there in the angle of his jaw, the darkening of his eyes and the way his lips curved just so. "Good to know," she managed. "I'm sure she can help you do that."

"Perfect, because I really want to spend some time with her." As the moment hovered, he straightened and returned to the reason they were here in Dallas—the showcase. "We have the opening cocktail party in two hours. Shall we reconvene this conversation in say fifty minutes so we can get downstairs? Just knock when you're ready." With that, he began to close the door, and Rachel snapped to attention and did the same. Then she paused, for he had. "What are you wearing?" he asked.

"I brought a black sheath that I was going to wear tonight. I'll dress it up more for the award ceremony and dance."

He shook his head. "That won't do."

She bristled. "What do you mean that won't do? Black sheaths are classic. Like Audrey Hepburn." And it was all she had.

"The dance is far more formal. Not floor length, but you definitely need something with more sequins than a plain black sheath. People will be anywhere from semi-formal to black tie on Sunday. And tonight both men and women will be in designer cocktail attire. The rodeo champs really clean up and get fancy."

"I don't have any of that. I haven't had much need for glamour in the past eighteen months when my best accessory is a burp cloth draped over my shoulder."

He stepped into his suite and gestured for her to follow. He reached into his wallet and withdrew the company credit card. "Take this. Go downstairs to the boutique and ask for Laura."

She kept her hands by her side. "This is not *Pretty Woman*."

"No, it's not a movie because you're much prettier. But you represent our company, and you'll be by my side. If it's not too much to ask, I need you to dress for the event, not the man. You could wear a sackcloth and be perfect in my eyes, but I won't be the only one there. Besides, think of it as a trade-off. The hotel won't charge for these rooms because of their mistake so they're paying for your dresses."

His compliments and logic touched her, but she still

tried to make sense of her conflicting feelings. Reaching for her hand, he pressed the credit card into it. He folded her fingers around the flat plastic, and his touch lingered on her skin seconds longer than necessary, creating warmth and reassurance. "Trust me…you deserve this."

"I'm paying you back," she insisted.

"No, you're not. Remember what I said about the hotel? And get it out of your head that using this card means you're a gold digger. My dad was wrong about you, so don't let him get to you. When you walk into the party tonight, you'll see why your wardrobe for the weekend is a business expense. Now go. Enjoy yourself and do not worry about the price. I'm going to call and find out why our luggage hasn't arrived yet. Seriously, they need to do better or we'll be moving locations next year."

As she made her way to the hall, Oakley was already on the room phone. She stepped into the elevator. One of the latest retail trends was for luxury hotels to have a series of high-end boutiques, and she found one conveniently located off the ornate lobby.

Despite her hesitation of an actual *Pretty Woman* rejection moment, the sales force greeted her warmly. Soon they had her measured and seated on a velvet divan with a glass of champagne in her hand while they pulled a bunch of dresses and underthings that cost more per piece than Rachel's monthly utilities. Then she went into a plush dressing room larger than her kitchen.

First, she tried on a jewel-neck, sleeveless cotton-blend dress in lipstick red. The fit and flare silhouette ended in a scalloped hem that fell right below her knees. "It's made in Italy," the saleswoman said when Rachel stepped out to show her. "Everyone always thinks cocktail parties mean wearing black, but you'll discover that women who have your slim figure and confidence will wear something more flattering than basic black. This color is perfect on you."

It was, and she'd never seen anything so pretty. "This must have been how Cinderella felt," Rachel said as she ran her fingers over the floral lace that lay over the skin-colored lining. She would wear this tonight. "This is an incredible dress. I'll take it."

"Excellent. I suggest this one next, for the award ceremony and the ball. You'll go from red to this."

"I'm sensing that floral is a theme," Rachel said as she slid into a sleeveless, metallic fil coupé midi-dress. The base of the dress was gray, with silver threads creating unique, raised freeform flowers. The dress shimmered and she gasped.

"Another winner," the saleswoman gushed. "Has just enough Western flair meets Gilded Age. With matching shoes, he won't be able to take his eyes off you."

"Oh, that's not why..."

The saleswoman helped Rachel out of the dress. "If you don't have a man, you'll certainly have them flocking to you when they see you wearing these dresses. Now, let's find you some work outfits, and some shoes, too. Don't worry...we'll be sure they fit so you're comfortable from the start. You may feel like Cinderella, but no need to lose a shoe, am I right?"

When Rachel returned to her room, she was loaded down with everything from new jeans to slacks to tops and the dresses. She had so many things the bellhop had to help her carry the large number of shopping bags. A bit tight on time, she opened her suitcase—thank goodness it had been delivered—and began getting ready by brushing her hair smooth. Once she was in the dress she'd twist her hair into a French knot.

Sliding into silky undergarments no one would see seemed indulgent, and while she thought it silly, she let herself enjoy how good they felt. The dresses spoke for themselves and didn't require much jewelry, meaning her own simple locket on a chain was the perfect complement. Playing dress-up had never been so fun.

There was only one problem. Down in the boutique she'd had someone to zip her. After wiggling awhile and trying to reach behind her back, she opened her door to Oakley's suite and knocked. "Come in," he called.

She stepped into his space and passed by the dining area. "I need help with my zipper. I can't get the last of it." She stopped explaining as she noted his fingers had frozen while adjusting a cufflink. She pointed to his wrist. "Do you need help with that?"

He shook himself. "No. I got it. Let's get you zipped."

She turned around and used both hands to lift her hair. The teeth of the zipper locked as he lifted the tab. His fingers brushed the back of her neck as he hooked the clasp. A sensual shiver ran down her spine.

"You're good," he said, the words sounding far away, as if they'd caught in his throat.

Something uncharacteristic made her give an impulsive twirl. "You like?"

He took two steps back. "Yes. It's a great color on you." He fixed his cuff and lowered his eyelids, but not before she'd seen the desire reflected there.

The saleswoman had been accurate. The dress had "wow" factor. "How about I meet you downstairs in the ballroom? I want to check on a few things, anyway."

"If you're sure. I won't be that far behind." An unspoken spark of heightened awareness traveled between them. If he weren't her boss, she'd cross the space and throw herself into his arms.

"I'm sure." Pulling the door closed behind her, Rachel escaped barefoot back to her room. She drew a steadying breath. If Oakley kept looking at her like that, she'd start believing that fantasies came true. He looked delicious in his tux, which fit him perfectly. As she slid her feet into the designer heels, she reminded herself to tread carefully.

Cinderella needed to remember to keep her shoes on and try not to fall for the sexy, desirable and most generous prince.

Chapter Ten

Oakley hadn't quite believed it could be true when someone said, "She took my breath away." That was until he'd seen Rachel walk out wearing that red dress and found himself unable to breathe, much less find a way to make a coherent sentence. She'd been the sexiest, most beautiful woman he'd ever seen. The color flattered her skin tone. The style enhanced her figure rather than exposing it, creating a mystery he wanted to unravel and explore. When he'd accidentally grazed her neck as he'd zipped her dress, it was like he'd touched an electric current—the zing had been so palpable. He didn't care what amount she'd put on the company credit card—every penny had been worth it, seeing her in that gorgeous dress. She made his heart race.

The elevator doors opened and he stepped out onto the ballroom level. Guests had started arriving at the cocktail party, which was an invite-only event that officially kicked off the weekend. He greeted the Fortune Rodeo Corporation employees staffing the check-in table before entering the ballroom. He spotted Rachel immediately. She was hard to miss—a bright speck of red in a sea of mostly black or dark blue. She was standing with Hannah, his Vice President of Public Relations and social media dynamo. Both turned in his direction as he approached.

"Looks like it's going to be another successful event," Hannah murmured. "I was telling Rachel that we've sold out tickets for Friday and Saturday nights. I've had celebrity assistants calling me all day to secure a spot. Don't worry, I found them some."

"That's fantastic." Oakley watched as more people flowed into the ballroom. Owing to the nature of the competitions starting the next morning, most of the rodeo cowboys in attendance wouldn't drink much alcohol tonight. The bar tab would be far higher for Sunday's awards dinner and gala when the competitors let loose. Tonight was mostly about mingling—agents, managers, judges, participants, stock owners and wranglers. The event would end with the drawing of the names matching each contestant to his first round animal. The event was mostly ceremonial, as the rest of the weekend's draws would be sent out electronically.

"I'm going to steal Rachel away if you don't mind," Oakley told Hannah. "I want her to meet some of the other VPs and managers." He guided his admin toward a group of people. He found himself impressed as the introductions went on. Rachel knew how to handle herself in social situations, and she was excellent at making small talk, including drawing even the most introverted into warm and meaningful conversations.

Unable to stay by her side the entire night, he remained aware of where she was throughout. The cocktail party had heavy appetizers that could serve as dinner, but after the draw, most guests would leave to find something more substantial before retiring for the night. On Friday and Saturday, the public part of the showcase started at noon and went late into the evening, or until the last event ended. Sunday featured the final rounds.

"How's it going?" Oakley asked when he finally got another chance to speak with Rachel. Her enthusiasm was contagious.

"I've learned so much. I have a much better appreciation for all you do and how your company works. Everyone is so nice, and I've enjoyed meeting them. Speaking of, here comes Clark. He said I should call him that."

"And you should." Oakley turned to face his second-in-command. After saying hello, Rachel slipped away. Both men watched her go.

"Now that I've met her, I can see what the fuss is about," Clark observed. Oakley didn't like the speculative gleam he saw in his best friend's eyes.

"So what? I made a fuss. Big deal. She's worked hard and deserves to be recognized and introduced to people."

"Nice attempt at a save, but what I meant is that I can tell that you're into her and I can understand why." Clark had the gall to grin.

Oakley and Clark had been friends since their senior year of high school and all through college. When Oakley started his company, he knew he had to have Clark at his side. The two men had known each other long enough that Clark could see right through any of Oakley's attempts to deny his growing feelings for Rachel. Across the way, Rachel began talking to one of the young rodeo champions and he felt a flicker of jealousy. "Is it obvious?"

"Only to me and only because I know you so well." Clark followed Oakley's gaze. "And you shouldn't worry about Rachel. She can hold her own with Cody Fallsworth." Clark reached his arm out and gathered the woman who approached to his side. She snuggled to him.

"What's only to you?" Clark's wife, Olivia, asked as she settled in. "I caught part of that conversation."

"Oakley is smitten with his admin," Clark told her. "He's jealous of Cody Fallsworth."

"Rachel? Really?" Olivia didn't appear too shocked. She craned her neck so she could see Rachel and Cody, who were now deep in an animated conversation. Oakley's jealousy spiked, and he tamped it down. He had no claim over Rachel or her time. She was her own woman and could talk to whomever she wished, including rodeo's biggest star, whose inordinate amount of male interest was obvious. *Damn that dress and its magical powers.* She'd already bewitched Oakley—did he have to fight every man in the room for her attentions?

"I haven't yet met Rachel," Olivia said. "I love that red dress she's got on. She's really pretty. You could do a lot worse, Oakley."

"He already has," Clark reminded both of them.

"Enough. Rachel and I are professional work colleagues. You know better than anyone the rules and pitfalls of interoffice relationships."

Olivia grinned. "Yes, you declare it with HR like we did. Then you fall in love and get married and have two kids and a dog." Olivia pressed her hand gently against Clark's chest so she could give him a kiss on the lips. As she used her thumb to wipe away the smudge of lipstick, Oakley found himself envious. Clark had been married for five years now. Oakley had thought that he and his wife would keep pace with his friends. They'd both have their kids around the same time and do all the things couples did with their couple friends.

But fate, it seemed, had other plans.

"You two worked in different departments, so you had

to make an effort to see each other," he pointed out. "Rachel and I work in a small, two-person office. We are in constant contact daily. I walk right by her desk on the way to mine. If things go wrong, how awkward would that be? I can't risk destroying our professional relationship because of some attraction or chemistry." He knew Rachel agreed with him. She'd been the one to say it couldn't be more.

Her headshake signaled Olivia's disagreement. "You set the ground rules early. If you feel she could be more than that initial chemistry, that your relationship could be far deeper, then it might be worth the risk. It might even be easier, as you're out of the prying eyes of the Dallas office."

"She doesn't want that," Oakley protested. "She's said as much."

Both Clark's and his wife's eyes narrowed before they exchanged a glance with each other. "What happened?" Olivia asked.

"Who said anything happened?" Oakley said.

"You forget we know you," Clark said. "Spill."

Oakley shifted his weight. "We've had a couple of moments, and then there was this time we kissed…"

"*Oakley!*" Olivia gave him a whack on the arm.

"Ow," he said as he rubbed his coat sleeve.

Olivia was undaunted. "That's for not telling us first thing. We're your best friends. If you're in love with someone, you should be divulging these things ASAP."

"Who said anything about love?" And why did thinking about love in the context of Rachel not give him pause? Ensuring they couldn't be overheard, he leaned toward the couple and filled them in on the pertinent details. "So that's where things stand between us."

Olivia shook her head. "I don't know whether to admire her or throttle you both. It's so clear you adore her. You said she has a child?"

"Allie. She's the cutest thing ever. She's almost ten months." Oakley smiled at the memory of holding her.

"You've got it bad, pal." Clark clapped his hand on Oakley's shoulder. "This tells me she just might be the one."

"Let's all do dinner," Olivia suggested. "In fact, I'll arrange it."

Oakley interrupted before Olivia had him down the church aisle. "No, no. If you try to sing my praises, she'll go running for the hills. If things are going to happen, they'll be on our terms. Whatever *we* decide." Oakley found himself wanting things to happen and frustrated he couldn't push forward like he normally did. He desired the one woman who didn't return his emerging feelings, and her not doing so wasn't some game she was playing in an attempt to be coy. She had legitimate reasons—one of those her need for a paycheck.

Olivia pouted as she accepted Oakley's answer. "Fine. But we are going to hang out. This is my fun weekend away from the kids. Girls will be girls." She arched her eyebrows, trailed her fingers over her husband's shoulders and walked away.

"Great, she's up to something," Oakley muttered.

Clark chuckled, his love for his wife clear. Since she was in dark blue, Olivia disappeared into the remaining crowd. "She's a force of nature."

"And you married her," Oakley teased. He'd stood by Clark's side as his best man when he got married. His friend had found his soulmate, so some liberties could be taken.

"That I did, and I have no regrets. Not a one, including when she complains I forgot to put the toilet seat down."

"Depending on what she tells Rachel, I might have some regrets," Oakley said. "Somehow, I suspect whatever Olivia says is going to come back to haunt me."

"Most likely it will," Clark admitted. "But as long as it promotes your cause and doesn't damage your relationship, do you really care? You like her, Oakley, and I haven't seen you this invested in a long time."

Which was what worried him. The crowd parted, and he could see Olivia approaching Rachel. His best friend's wife was about to meddle. But if it won him Rachel? Oakley might just be okay with that.

Rachel could understand why Cody Fallsworth was a champion, an internet sensation and an international celebrity. She could also understand why Taylor found him so appealing. He had that extra something that made women swoon and men take notice. Rachel might be into him, too, if he wasn't always on the road to the next competition, and if Oakley hadn't kissed her and ruined her for other men.

That didn't mean she couldn't enjoy Cody's attention and flattery. He'd not only told his assistant to send Taylor some autographed merchandise, but he'd even video-called her. She had been so excited Rachel had worried the older woman might pass out. But fortunately, she hadn't, and when Cody had handed Rachel's phone back, Taylor had mouthed, "Thank you." Rachel would have liked to have seen Allie, but her daughter was already in bed.

"Thank you for doing that," she told Cody as she slipped her phone into her new handbag.

"Anytime. It's what makes this job fun. You weren't

asking for yourself, and that's rare." He had one of those megawatt grins the cameras loved. His entire face was one of proportion and symmetry, from the full lips to the square jaw and wide-set deep brown eyes. He had strong cheekbones, one of which had a thin jagged scar that simply added to his powerful mystique. She'd seen the way women hovered, but the assistant had kept them at bay so that Cody could talk to her. It was a heady sensation.

Rachel sipped some of the white wine a server had brought her. She hadn't eaten any of the appetizers, so she was feeling the giddy effects of wine and Cody's attentions. "I haven't followed the circuit in forever. My dad's the one who got me into it."

"Well, are you going to be cheering me on this weekend? You should."

She tried not to let her heart race, but it was automatic when around a man of Cody's caliber. She strove to play it cool. "Doesn't the showcase favorite have enough people calling his name? And how will that look if I'm playing favorites? What will all the other contestants think?"

"That you know a winner when you see them, same as I do." The corner of his lips lifted, along with his eyebrows. "Same as how you picked that dress, you pick me because I deliver."

She could live in this flattery, Rachel realized. It was easy banter, the type that made no promises beyond this moment. How long had it been since someone had paid her this kind of male attention, aside from Oakley, of course? His attention came with complications. Cody's came with nothing but the fun flirtation of no expectations.

"Rachel! Here you are!" A woman came up to her. "And Cody. How are you doing? You going to give the crowd another win? Your trophy shelves must be about to break from the weight of all the hardware you've brought home this year."

"You know it, Olivia." He saw Rachel's confusion and gave her a "can you believe we've been interrupted" roll of his eyes. "Rachel, this is Olivia Adams. Clark's wife. Olivia, you really need to stop assuming everyone knows who you are."

Olivia tittered and put her hand on her heart. "But, darling, they always do. Rachel simply hasn't met me yet. She spent all her time with Clark and Oakley, poor dear."

Rachel hadn't really spoken to Clark tonight either. But they had worked together during conference calls. "Nice to meet you, Olivia."

"I've come to snag you for dinner." Olivia gazed pointedly at Cody. "You weren't going to ask her, were you? The executive staff has a reservation and we assumed Rachel would be joining us."

If he had been going to ask her, Olivia had kiboshed that.

"Rachel, I can see you're busy," Cody said, and Rachel could see the hints of disappointment etched into his handsome features. "If your bosses don't give you an all-access pass, find my assistant and she'll give you one of mine. Remember, you're my cheering squad. I'm depending on you."

"I won't forget," Rachel promised as she let Olivia lead her away. "While it's nice to meet you, I didn't need saving," she told her.

Olivia gave a toss of her hair. "Oh, I know. If you had, Oakley would have come over himself. But you have made him green-eyed and that's a rare feat, one I'm down for."

Oakley could not be jealous. The thought thrilled Rachel anyway, which was wrong as she'd been the one to insist that things remain professional.

"There they are," Clark said as Rachel and Olivia approached.

"Taylor's favorite rider is Cody," Rachel said. "My daughter's caregiver," she explained when she saw Clark and Olivia's confusion. "He was generous enough to FaceTime her."

"Who? Allie?" Oakley asked.

"No, Taylor," Rachel clarified. "I was worried she'd faint and I'd have to go home."

"Good thing she didn't, since you're going to dinner with the three of us," Olivia said. "Clark and I insist. I made a reservation for four people. I'd like to get to know you. You run my husband's and best friend's lives, after all."

"Then how can I say no? Do we need to stay to the end?"

Oakley shook his head. "Nope. After I give my extremely short speech, we can leave. It's all Hannah's event after that."

They went somewhere both intimate and worthy of the dresses they were wearing, a place with low lighting, heavy wood tables covered with white linen and plush, leather armchairs. Rachel sat to Oakley's right, and across from her was Olivia. That allowed them to talk throughout dinner. The five-course chef's menu with a main course of roasted duck proved the place lived up to its starred rating.

"I like your friends," she said when she and Oakley returned to the penthouse level. She hadn't laughed so hard in years. Olivia's sense of humor had kept the conversation flowing. At no point had Rachel felt like she was out with her bosses, but rather with good friends.

"They liked you, too," Oakley assured her. "Let me help you with your dress. Unless you think you can undo it?"

"Probably not." No one was in the hallway, so he followed her into her room. Her breath caught as he unhooked the clasp and lowered the zipper to a respectable level. "Thanks for an enjoyable evening, Rachel. Sleep well."

Then he was gone, back through the connecting door into his suite so fast that she wasn't sure the whiplash was real or imagined. She shut the door and threw the lock, mainly out of habit than anything else. She knew Oakley wouldn't try to come into her room. He was too much of a gentleman for that. But what did she want to happen anyway? She'd been the one to tell him any relationship would be impossible.

She hung the gown up and put on her pajamas. Her phone beeped with a text. Thinking it might be Oakley, she swiped.

It was from a number she didn't recognize. She read the text: Save me a dance Sunday. And don't forget to cheer for me.

Cody. He must have gotten her number when they called Taylor. She hearted his message.

As her conflicting feelings offered no answers or respite, it was the least she could do.

Chapter Eleven

The weekend had gone better than Rachel could have imagined. By Sunday night, she was truly enjoying herself. She'd watched rodeo events from the special boxes reserved for Oakley's employees. With her all-access pass, she'd even made her way into the participant areas. She'd spoken to Cody once or twice, but mostly in passing as they were both busy, and he was concentrating on the competition. Olivia had also taken her under her wing. Rachel had met so many people that by the time the awards ceremony banquet and dance rolled around, she felt she knew almost everyone.

As she'd been doing each evening, Rachel sat next to Oakley during the awards dinner. Tonight the ten people at their banquet table were lively. The evening's host sat with them, and he was a comedian who would do a short opening set before announcing the results Oscar-style. The competitors knew their times and places, so receiving their buckles and prize money was mostly ceremonial. Rachel discovered that the hour-long presentation was a fun tradition everyone in the grand ballroom enjoyed.

Once the awards were over, someone commanded Oakley's and Clark's attention, so Olivia snagged Rachel and drew her out onto the dance floor. "I don't get to do this much since Clark and I had kids. Dancing to 'Old MacDonald Had a Farm' is not the same. I plan to dance until my feet hurt."

"I'm surprised my feet don't already hurt," Rachel said. She scanned the room for Oakley but didn't see him. When she spotted him a short time later, he was speaking with a beautiful redhead who Rachel didn't recognize. The band ended one number and as the singer spoke to the crowd, Olivia followed Rachel's gaze. "Oh, her. You have nothing to worry about. Can't you see how this weekend he's only had eyes for you?"

Had he? He'd been warm and friendly, but he'd been that way with everyone. When they'd reached the penthouse, he'd gone into his room and she into hers like the professional work colleagues they were.

"I wasn't worrying, and I think you're imagining things. I was seeing if he needed rescue. I promised I'd do that."

Olivia snorted. "Believe me, Oakley can rescue himself. He's not been this invested in someone until he…" Olivia stopped. "Sorry. Listen to me ramble."

Rachel saw the telltale, guilty flush. "Until what? What are you insinuating? That Oakley wants something from me?"

"No, that's not what I meant."

"Did he tell you what happened?" Rachel demanded.

Olivia wouldn't meet her eyes. "He said the two of you were keeping things professional."

So, he *had* told his friends about the kiss.

"Clark and I met at work," Olivia added helpfully. "And we only want to see Oakley happy. He's a great guy, Rachel. He likes you—I know it. Give him a chance."

"He is a great guy," Rachel agreed, "which is why we

have to keep things simple and work-related." That meant that she shouldn't be feeling this flare of jealousy as Oakley laughed at something the redhead said. "I have too much to lose if we don't."

"I know. I understand…and I won't bring it up again." Olivia winked. "Oh, and FYI… Cody Fallsworth is walking this way and that movie star smile is just for you."

He greeted her with a dimpled grin that had the power to render women speechless, as proved by the one attendant fanning herself nearby after he passed through her group of friends. "Miss Evers."

"Mr. Fallsworth." Adrenaline couldn't help but pulse through her.

"As my number one cheerleader, would you do me the honor of the next dance?"

Rachel was highly aware of Olivia's avid interest. "Seeing as you did win the grand prize during tonight's ceremony, how could I say no?"

"I'd say the real prize tonight is you. You are stunning in that dress. Silver is another color that suits you." Cody's appreciative gaze stayed above her neckline, which made her respect him even more.

"And you, Mr. Fallsworth, are a flatterer."

"You deserve to be flattered." He reached for her hands, which she let him take. Touching him didn't create an electric sensation, not like when she touched Oakley. He led her deeper into the crowd on the dance floor. Rachel glanced over her shoulder, but Olivia was nowhere to be seen.

Cody was a great dancer, so she couldn't help but have fun. One song led into two, then three, and when they left the dance floor, she discovered his drink of choice to be club soda with lime. "I had some champagne earlier. One's always my limit, and that was my one."

"I rarely drink, unless I'm out with people." She still had most of the bottle of wine Jenny had brought over the day she'd first quit working for Oakley. "I have a nine-month-old, and while I'm no longer nursing, when I was I didn't drink at all. Or for the nine months I was pregnant either. Then it simply became unnecessary except on rare occasions."

"I find it dulls my nervous system. I practice and work out every day, so I'd rather be sharp. It's dangerous being on the back of the bull."

He'd drawn one of the toughest animals. "You made it look easy."

"Eight seconds can seem like an eternity when the ride goes bad. My dad taught me that. The key is doing everything in your power to ensure the ride doesn't go bad."

"That's a good philosophy. Your dad sounds wise."

"He is." With that, they talked about their families, and Cody shared how his niece was around Allie's age. The more they talked, the more Rachel relaxed.

She knew nothing would come from her time with Cody, but for the night, until they parted ways, it was wonderful to bask in Cody's attention. He was fun and flirty, and handsome, and she saw the envious looks of other women. Despite traveling nonstop, he should be the kind of guy she should fall for. But she'd met Oakley first. His kiss had set a new standard, and she wasn't yet in the place where she wanted to kiss anyone else and have it fail to reach expectations. Of course, Cody might be able to shatter that record like he'd done others this weekend, but as much as he was sexy and attentive, if she were honest with herself, she wanted Oakley. Having joined Cody in sipping a club soda, Rachel took a drink so Cody couldn't tell her attention had wandered to another man.

"Another dance?" The band had started a slow number, which the singer announced was their second to last song of the night. Rachel followed Cody to the dance floor, where he placed his hands in the appropriate places on her lower back. They swayed to the music and held whispered conversations until, when the music ended, Cody drew back as someone tapped his shoulder. Rachel saw Oakley standing there.

"Mind if I cut in?" he asked. "Rachel promised to save me one dance, and it's the last song."

If Cody minded, he ceded gracefully. He touched the brim of his Stetson. "Rachel. Nice meeting you. You have my number. Feel free to use it."

She watched as he melted into the crowd. "Do you mind my cutting in?" Oakley ventured. "Cody assumed I was speaking to him when it was also your call. I didn't realize you too had gotten so close. I can let you go after him if you'd like—"

"No," Rachel said honestly. The difference in the way Oakley's hands settled onto her waist spoke volumes. Cody was an attractive, gorgeous man, but his touch hadn't stirred the same passionate responses that Oakley's did. With Oakley, she wanted to close the gap, to press herself against him and inhale the woodsy aphrodisiac that was his aftershave. Aware they were in public, she did neither.

"You and Cody seemed to hit it off," Oakley muttered, and if the band wasn't playing, Rachel swore she might have heard a hint of jealousy. It shouldn't thrill her, but it did.

"He's a nice guy. I heard some people calling him a

player, but I didn't see any of that. He was perfectly respectable. Do you know he has one drink and that's it? Can't say that about some of the other rodeo guys."

"No, you can't." Oakley shifted his hands so they didn't drift lower. "We had a few overindulge, but it ended up okay. They're upstairs in their rooms sleeping it off."

"I'm sure this is like a big wedding reception where people let loose and let down their hair, especially after competing as hard as they do."

Upon hearing the word hair, Oakley tucked some of her loose strands behind her ear, the gesture intimate. "I like when you wear yours down."

Rachel swallowed hard. The singer crooned the last words as the band played the final notes. After a thank you, piped music came through the hotel speakers. Rachel stepped out of Oakley's arms. "Thank you for the dance."

"You're welcome." The lights slowly brightened. "Unlike Thursday night, I usually stay until the end of the gala, but you can escape if you want."

"No, I'll stay. I want to see how things unfold." While she meant she wanted to see how an event such as his wrapped, her words definitely came out with a double meaning. What would happen between them if she stayed by his side? Despite her resolve, she'd developed feelings for him and was falling for him. She warned herself to be careful. It would be too easy to lose the rest of her heart.

Maybe the seeds had been planted all along, but they'd truly sprouted when he'd defended her to his father. Add in the dinners and meetings, and the lines between them had blurred.

She glanced around but there was no sign of Cody. Just as well, she thought. She didn't want to explain that nothing would happen between them. Olivia approached. "I wanted to tell you both that Clark and I are making our escape. It was so wonderful to meet you, and I hope we get to see much, much more of you."

"It was nice to meet you, too," Rachel said, accepting Olivia's hug.

"Give him a chance, okay?" Olivia whispered as Clark came to retrieve her and her husband spent a couple of seconds speaking to Oakley. "He's worth the effort."

Rachel wished she were in a place where she could risk her heart. She waited while Oakley made his final rounds. People loved him. But how could they not? Her pulse quickened as he walked toward her. "Ready?" he said.

"Yeah." She followed him to the elevator, which whisked them to the penthouse level.

Rachel removed her keycard. "Would you like a nightcap?" Oakley asked as they walked down the hall. "I find it takes some time for me to wind down, so the butler left some chamomile tea brewing. There's also some assorted nuts if you'd like to partake."

She felt the same wired tension he did. "Some tea actually sounds wonderful. If you don't mind?"

"Of course not. Just come through when you're ready."

With that, he unlocked his door and stepped inside. Rachel went into her room, kicked off her heels and opened the interior door between their rooms. She stepped through, joining him. Rachel tried to ignore how housekeeping had unfolded the couch into a bed. Oakley had thrown his suit coat over the back of an armchair.

He was in the kitchen, and he came out carrying a tray covered with two ceramic teapots, a plate of nuts, and some soft pitas and hummus. There were also a few chocolate truffles and an assortment of shortbread cookies, and two bottles of water. He set the tray on the dining room table.

Rachel's stomach rumbled as he helped her into a chair. "That looks good."

"It's all the butler or kitchen staff. That's one reason I like this hotel, when it's not canceling reservations, that is." He passed her a small dessert plate and a cup. When she reached forward, the mirror on the wall showed how the dress shimmered. She caught him staring.

His lips lifted guiltily. "I do love that dress."

"Me too. I almost don't want to take it off. Speaking of, I'll need your help with the zipper later."

"I can do that." He pointed to the teapots. "That's the chamomile and that's the hibiscus."

"I'll take the hibiscus." She reached for the pot and poured the crimson-colored water into the teacup. "I've always liked fruit teas. Lemon-flavored are good, too."

He poured the chamomile tea into his cup. "This one works like magic and will help me sleep. Thanks for sitting with me. Helps me burn off the energy from the night."

"It was a great evening," Rachel said. "Everything was so well done this weekend."

"We did have a few hiccups," Oakley reminded her. "You had to deal with a few minor mishaps, like when the programs didn't arrive on time."

"Yes, but nothing that wasn't quickly resolved. You have great people working for you who love their jobs and it shows. It made my part easy."

"Do you enjoy your job?" Oakley asked curiously.

"I do," Rachel confirmed. "I've had a great few weeks and am looking forward to many more."

"That's good to hear." Oakley reached for some almonds and chewed thoughtfully. "I want you to be happy. The office will grow once I make a permanent commitment to relocate everyone. It's such a process. Fortunately, Clark and Olivia's kids aren't in school yet."

"What about relocating the headquarters to Emerald Ridge and keeping a satellite office in Dallas? You could let those who want to relocate move over the course of the next year rather than do a huge move that feels rushed."

"That's a good idea. I've been actually toying around with it and would love to hear more about your suggestion. But not tonight. Work topics are banned."

"Then what's left?" She discovered the chocolate was delicious.

"Allie? How was she when you checked in on her?"

Rachel spread some hummus on a pita. "Great. Taylor said she's had no issues and that she had a ball at the family picnic. She sent pictures." She popped the bite into her mouth and reached for her phone. She scrolled to the pictures. "See?"

Oakley leaned into her space. "Look at her. So cute. She's having so much fun."

"She was. My baby girl loved the bubbles." Rachel swiped to show him more pictures.

"I'm glad you didn't have to worry."

"Taylor's been a godsend. Have you ever hit it off with someone immediately? Like you knew you'd be friends and could see yourself with them long term?"

"Yes. You." The words hovered in the air. Then he reached for a shortbread cookie. "Ignore that. We're being professional."

"We can say we hit it off professionally. We work very well together," Rachel said, trying to release him from the faux pas.

Oakley groaned. “We weren’t going to talk about work, and obviously I can’t hold a conversation without making things personal. What about that weather we’re having? We got lucky this weekend, huh?”

She appreciated what he was trying to do. “We can be friends,” she said. “And on that note, since we have brunch in the morning, perhaps we should call it a night. But I am going to eat another of these chocolate truffles first.”

“I’ll be sure they box them up so you can take them with you when we leave.”

She took the last sip of tea before Oakley offered her his hand. Taking it steadied her as she stood.

“Zipper?” he asked.

“Yes, please.” She lifted the hair off her neck and presented him her back. He unhooked the clasp and slid the zipper down. She heard his hiss of breath as he stopped above her bra strap.

“Sorry.” His husky voice revealed he was as affected as she.

Rachel turned. His eyes had darkened and his jaw twitched. “Oakley.” To her own ears his name on her lips sounded like a plea.

“I’m holding on by a thread,” he admitted. “You have to know how much I want you. I don’t think I’ve ever been so jealous of a man as I was of Cody tonight. He got all the dances.”

“Except the last one.”

“I wanted to be the *only* one,” he told her, his desire clear. “I know it’s wrong and that’s not what you want.”

The only thing she wanted was his lips on hers, and while it might be a mistake, she had the feeling that if she didn’t kiss him, she’d regret it. She’d probably regret it either way, so why not risk a little? Her mom had once said that life was too short not to eat the cupcake, that tomorrow wasn't guaranteed.

"Kiss me," she told him, her arms weaving their way around his neck. Unlike their first kiss, which had been a cataclysmic crashing of two souls destined to meet, this one started far gentler. It was an exploration in restraint, a tender expedition of nipping and suckling and teasing. She tasted and savored. She inhaled his breath, let his tongue caress hers. Time was a friend, allowing them to enjoy the journey without worrying about the destination. Her hands threaded through his hair, while his circled the curve of her waist, fingers tracing the raised threads of the shimmery flowers before slipping beneath the fabric to stroke the skin of her back. When she met his gaze, his desirous eyes reflected her own hunger. He wanted her as much as she wanted him.

Before he spoke, she silenced him with another kiss, going even deeper. Her heartbeat pounded in her chest, the thump-thump matching the pace of his. She was teetering on the edge of something she couldn't stop or take back, nor did she want to. Unlike with Mitch, this was different. Definitely better, and totally delicious and decadent. She wanted him for more than passion. His sexiness went beyond his looks. It came from his kindness. The way he put others first. How he cared for his family. The way he treated Allie. He was the total package—handsome looks and a generous and loving heart.

Longing flowed through her as he slid her dress from her shoulders until it pooled at her waist. She stood in the silver lace bra the saleswoman had insisted she buy, and Rachel was grateful for her insight as Oakley sucked in a ragged breath. "You are so beautiful. I want you so much," he rasped, and hearing the trembling urgency, Rachel believed him.

She'd never thought of herself as beautiful before, more like average at best. Yet right here, right now, she felt boldly confident as he traced one of the thin stretch marks with his fingertips. He kissed a trail along her neck, then his hand came and cupped her breast through the lace.

His magical touch lit something inside her, stoked a fire from the embers of that past into something that raged through her. His kiss captured her lips and her tongue couldn't help but want more, darting into his mouth to explore the taste of him, which was wine and whiskey and all things delicious male. He only pulled his mouth from hers to slide his lips down over her flesh, finding her breasts. Her bra fell to the floor. Her chest rose to meet his exploration and her hands clung to his back.

"I want you," he said. "I want your skin on mine. Your body beneath me."

The part of her brain that screamed that this wasn't wise found itself overruled. "Yes."

His hand massaged her lower back, the electrifying tingles shooting from head to toe. "You're sure?"

"Yes." She would figure things out in the morning. Worry about tomorrow then. Tonight she felt as if she might die if she didn't have him, which while sounding extreme fit. She wanted to heighten the heat burning between him. Feel him everywhere. She began to undo the buttons on his shirt, revealing a rock-hard, sculpted chest begging to be touched. She dropped her lips to his smooth skin, delighting in his sharp intake of breath. Her fingers moved lower, wanting to feel all of him. She explored his body, until he took back over and scooped her into his arms. He lay her gently on the bed and stripped her bare.

"Comfortable?"

"I'd be more so if I wasn't the only one naked."

"Greedy. I like that." Seconds later, he joined her under the covers. His lips found hers again and they kissed deeply as his fingers slid between her legs. She bucked as one finger entered and then two. Her back arched and her head pressed into the pillow as he murmured encouragement. "There you go."

Her legs shook as she came, but he wasn't done, and lifting his lips from hers, he slid down to place his mouth where his fingers were.

She turned into putty in his hands. When he finally protected them, she was wet, slick and ready. He held her gaze as he entered her, the moment as fragile as it was desperate for satiation. They couldn't go back. She nodded, and then he was inside and moving. She clung to him, for it hadn't been like this before. Never had she been in sync with someone as she was with Oakley in this moment. She could hear the thumping of his heart, feel the blood in her veins with each stroke. She could see the tension on his face, the way he held himself taut with determination to give her more pleasure than he'd take for himself. "It's okay. Let go," she urged, and when he did, their bodies took over and took them to a place beyond where Rachel had ever orgasmed before. He held her tight afterward before he shifted and brushed the hair from her face. 'I'll be right back," he said.

And he was, before the shyness could come. He drew her into his arms. "You are a temptress, Rachel. The most beautiful temptress who's got me under her spell. I want you to know this is more than us slaking some of our base desires."

"We can't pretend this never happened," she said.

"No, we can't. If we're going to continue to do this, then we do it right or we don't do it at all. And right now, with everything going on, I'm worried I'm going to destroy us."

"Because you were hurt by your ex?" she asked softly.

"Yes. And because I don't want to lose you, and that's what happens when I get into serious relationships. And it has nothing to do with my dad, either. I don't care what he says. It's about what I *feel*."

"And what you feel is complicated," Rachel finished for him.

"Yes." Oakley was at least honest about that, which allowed her to respect him despite the hurt it caused. She'd made love to him, not just had *sex*. But perhaps the bright side was that the hurt would be far less now than if she kissed him again and they ended up making love again. "You're my admin. What if we don't work out? Both of us don't have exceptional track records."

"No, we don't." Sadness consumed her. The one relationship that might be perfect was the one that held the power to hurt the most. Finding out Oakley had feelings but didn't want to act on them was truly bittersweet. She'd broken the promise to Jenny that she wouldn't fall for him, or try to be the next Mrs. Fortune. The sobering truth was his father would never accept her. It was foolish to dream big.

"How about we just focus on being boss and admin," she suggested. "We say this was a one and done. Nothing more. Shall I meet you downstairs tomorrow? Brunch at ten?" she asked, making her tone more nonchalant than she felt.

"Rachel, don't," he pleaded. "Don't make this situation between us harder than it already is."

"I'm attempting to keep things professional because you're right. While I like you and you like me, it would be a mistake to do this again. I let myself get carried away, maybe because Olivia kept putting ideas into my head. Although, I can't blame her. She encouraged me to act on my feelings. I mean, it's obvious how happy she and Clark are. I want that."

"So do I," Oakley said. He touched her arm lightly.

She shrugged his hand off and slid out of bed. "But it's complicated since I need this job and you need a good admin. Let's let work be our priority. I'm going to use the bathroom. I'll see you in the morning."

She made no attempt to cover up and she kept her head high as she entered her bathroom and shut the door. Oakley was gone and the connecting door closed when she returned. She shook her head to stop the tears. She would not cry. She would not think about how she'd once again slept with someone she worked with, or how this time meant so much more than when she was with Mitch.

She hung the magical dress carefully and put on her pajamas. Tonight had been perfect, until it wasn't, and the letdown was immense. It should be so simple to have everything, have that cake and the icing, too.

As she removed her makeup, Cinderella turned back into ordinary old Rachel, mom and admin.

Her priority had to be her daughter, and to support her daughter, she needed this job. Making love to Oakley, no matter how wonderful or passionate, had been a mistake.

Making love to Rachel still bothered Oakley days later. He had no excuse for losing control the way he had. He'd wanted her, and he'd let himself take what he wanted.

The thing was, he didn't know what he wanted beyond

what they'd done. She deserved a man who would take her on dates and shower her with gifts and affection. Although, in a sense, the weekend had felt like a date, and he had previously showered her with gifts. He remained as confused as ever.

While the office wasn't tense, the dynamic had changed. He missed the friendly smiles she'd once directed his way. He wanted to hear her light laughter in response to something that he said.

Even Cheyenne noticed his discontent. When she arrived to the office for their visit with Kate Fortune, the moment they'd left she'd told him he was a big grump and he needed to snap out of whatever it was. By blaming it on missing Mewington, Oakley had managed to brush off her concerns as they climbed into the car. After all, all the siblings were worried about their dad's cat.

Oakley had seen pictures of Kate, but they'd never met. Last July, Clemons had crashed Kate's hundredth birthday party. It had been quite the scene when their father had announced he was the secret half brother of the late Archibald Fortune.

From doing his research, Oakley knew some of her backstory, which he told Cheyenne as they drove to a newer, gated lake community on the outskirts of town.

"She survived a plane crash," he said as they wound through the subdivision of half-acre homesites. "She pretended she was dead to expose the person who was trying to kill her and sabotage her company, Fortune Cosmetics."

"I've heard rave reviews of the Fortune Youth Serum," Cheyenne replied. "Our mom always wanted to try it. In every picture I've seen lately, Kate doesn't look one hundred. It's probably digital altering. No one can look that good at her age," Cheyenne added as they reached a large, single-story house. "Oh, this is pretty!"

"It is," Oakley said. It was the kind of place he'd like to own, an abode large enough to raise a family yet still feel homey. While a newer build, the house incorporated native limestone wainscoting and had multiple gabled sections of varying heights. The central wing featured a large peak with exposed wooden beams, and a covered porch spanned most of the front. He parked on an aggregate driveway. The yard was well tended and landscaped.

To their surprise, Kate opened her own door and proved that everything he'd heard about her independence was true. A walking advertisement for her product, she looked decades younger despite using a pearl-studded cane. "Come in, come in," she snapped as she stepped backward. "You're letting the air conditioning out. Resources aren't finite and I've always been a good steward of them."

"Yes, ma'am." Oakley entered the fourteen-foot-high foyer. A mahogany center table contained a bouquet of fresh roses. "Thank you for meeting with us."

Instead of taking them to the great room with its phenomenal view of the lake, Kate led them into the formal living room. She sat in a tall, throne-like wingback armchair fitting for the closest thing Texas had to royalty. She gestured, and Oakley and Cheyenne sat on the sofa. "My assistant will bring in a tea service. I've been curious since you contacted me. Tell me more about this Johnny Doe."

"He's an amnesiac Oakley found along the Emerald Ridge River promenade. He's still in the hospital." Cheyenne gave Kate the most recent information. "He's in stable condition and soon to begin the rehabilitation phase where they'll work with him on memory retraining exercises."

"Who knew a bump on the noggin could do so much damage," Kate mused. Her assistant came in carrying a tray with a large teapot and three cups. After pouring, the assistant distributed the cups and left.

Kate lifted her cup, and Oakley followed suit, finding she'd served a lemon and ginger blend. The tea was the perfect temperature, and drinking it reminded him of the time at the hotel with Rachel. Melancholy must have shown on his face, for Kate said, "Penny for your thoughts." Her mind and powers of observation remained razor-sharp.

Oakley used the point of their visit to get his mind off Rachel. "I was wondering if you knew anything about our father's past that might help us identify Johnny Doe. He had a picture on him, but we don't know who the baby in the photo is, or why he knew my dad's name."

"I brought a copy." Cheyenne took a sheet of paper from her purse and handed it to Kate, who studied the picture carefully before passing it back.

"I wish I could help you, but I don't recognize that baby," Kate said.

The assistant returned carrying a three-tiered serving tray filled with finger sandwiches and sweets. Kate reached for a savory and again indicated Oakley and Cheyenne should help themselves. "There is something that rings a bell about the photo, but I can't say what. I'm sorry I'm not more help. I've seen dozens of baby pictures over the years and they do all blend together after a while. I am one hundred, after all."

"That's what I said, but I don't exactly see many babies. I don't have my own family yet." Oakley sipped more tea.

"You should get on that," Kate told him, a sharp twinkle in her eyes. "You're not getting any younger."

“That’s what I keep telling him,” Cheyenne added, piling on. She winked at him before innocently sipping more tea.

“Trying,” Oakley deadpanned. Changing the subject, he circled back to his father. “I also wanted to apologize for our dad crashing your party.”

Kate wiped her fingers on a square napkin. “Added some excitement,” she chuckled. “And as I told your dad, I didn’t know that Archibald had a younger brother who’d been put up for adoption. I met Archibald when he was a scrappy, ambitious eighteen-year-old who appeared in my office one day to ask for a loan. Did you know he’d once lived in barns?”

“I did not.” Oakley reached for a chocolate. He knew very little about Archibald.

“He charmed me, so I gave him a thousand dollars to chase his dream. He showed promise, and he built Fortune Airlines using hard work and gumption. His daughter, Madeline, planned my birthday party. I believe you have your own company, Oakley?” She tilted her head.

He had been absently staring at the comb holding one side of Kate’s silver hair back and was caught off guard. “Yes, Fortune Rodeo Corp. We held our huge championship showcase last weekend in Dallas.”

“Tell me more,” she suggested, and Oakley knew that the old woman didn’t have any more information on the baby picture Johnny Doe had had in his pocket, or if there might be a connection to Clemons. He and Cheyenne left after tea, and after Kate had assured them that if she remembered anything that might help them identify Johnny Doe and his connection to Clemons, she’d contact them immediately.

"She's nice," Cheyenne said. "I hope I'm that with it at age one hundred."

"Same." Oakley navigated his way back into town. "I just wish she'd had more answers. We're no closer than we were before." He pressed a button on the dash and asked Siri to call the hospital. The operator connected him to the lab, where he asked the lab nurse the status of his DNA test.

"Hello, Mr. Fortune," she said. "We're sorry we don't have those results yet. We understand you want to check on familial connection to Mr. Doe, but unfortunately, there's a backlog. It'll probably be a couple more weeks. It's marked high priority and we are doing the best we can."

Oakley thanked her for their time and ended the call. "See. Nowhere."

"Just like Dad's cat," Cheyenne lamented. "There have been multiple sightings and people keep calling the reward hotline, but nothing's panned out yet. It's sad and discouraging."

"I can't imagine how Dad feels—the not knowing." Oakley drummed his fingers on the steering wheel in a rapid staccato.

His sister peered at him. "This is more than your DNA test being delayed. What's got you tied in knots? Although, if I wager a guess, it has something to do with that pretty admin of yours."

"We kissed." Oakley couldn't keep it a secret any longer. He didn't add the rest of what they'd done.

"What?" Cheyenne turned in her seat to stare at him. "How long have you been holding on to that? I can't believe you didn't say anything."

"What can I say? That while it didn't feel like a mistake, it *is* a mistake? We can't mix business with pleasure. And she's worth so much more than some cheap fling."

"You're saying you wouldn't offer her anything more than a fling?" Cheyenne asked. "That's not like you."

"That's not what I'm saying. I'm saying she's the type of woman who deserves a real relationship. I'm her boss—I can't give her that." Because he was too focused on the company, he'd probably lose her like he'd lost his ex. Though it pained him, he couldn't be selfish and keep Rachel from finding happiness.

"You're looking at this wrong. You are the boss, Oakley. You can do whatever you want. You already have, when you offered to pay her more after she quit."

"Don't you think I haven't considered that?" he bit out. "You heard Evanston at dinner after I bought the baby stuff. He said it was inappropriate. I can't date her and be her boss. It doesn't work. Besides, my ex is proof I'm bad at relationships."

"You have always figured out how to do the impossible," Cheyenne said as he drove up to the hotel. "It's one reason I've always looked up to you. I'm rooting for you, whatever you choose to do. But if I were you, I'd figure out a way to have it all."

Could he? He simply needed to figure out how.

Chapter Twelve

Just because the rodeo showcase was over didn't mean things in the office slowed down, Rachel discovered. If anything, they continued at light speed as two more government entities reached out to see if Oakley's company would be interested in a partnership. One was a county in the southwestern part of the state. Officials there wanted to add a smaller-size, amateur competition to their local county fair. Another was a town closer to New Mexico that wanted to bring in tourists. A former professional bull rider had opened a ranch nearby and suggested reaching out. Oakley had also secured the contract for the Lubbock showcase.

As she finalized the contracts and emailed them to the Fortune Rodeo Corporation employees who would be traveling to Lubbock for the official signing, she leaned back after hitting Send. She was thrilled for Oakley. He'd worked so hard since Dallas to make things happen. He'd also thanked her multiple times.

Their lovemaking seemed a distant memory now that over a week had passed since Dallas. Oakley had been the perfect, professional boss, maintaining both physical and emotional distance. It was as if he'd put her in a compartment and shut the door.

She hated it. Daily she admired him more and more. She saw how hard he worked to take care of his family. They were no closer to getting answers about Johnny Doe and no closer to finding Mewington. Oakley was under enormous pressure and had the fine lines around his eyes to prove it. The last thing she wanted to do was add to his stress, so she hid her growing feelings. Instead, she worked to make his job go as smoothly as possible.

She still felt the loss of how they'd acted toward each other in Dallas. She'd thought things had been bad when Mitch had left—or when Clemons had sued her—but this was different and, in a way, worse. She'd met the man of her dreams, and too much stood in the way, including her own pride. Dating Oakley would confirm to his father that she was a gold digger, or that she was as bad as the woman who'd sat in this chair before her.

Speaking of, she hadn't stood all morning, which she tried to do once an hour to get the blood flowing. She went into the kitchen, grabbed a tall glass from the cabinet and, already overcaffeinated from her morning coffee, filled it with water. She was mid-sip when her phone trilled with the sound assigned to Taylor. She'd spoken with her neighbor about an hour ago. Frowning, she answered. "Hello? Taylor? Is something wrong?"

"Is this Rachel?"

A chill swept over her. She didn't recognize the voice. "Yes. Who's this? Why do you have Taylor's phone?"

"It's Lisa from the yoga studio. Taylor missed the last step and fell on her way out of the building. The paramedics are here but she's refusing to leave because of Allie. You need to come home."

"I'm on my way!" Rachel was in the process of throwing her things into her purse when Oakley appeared in the doorway.

"What's going on?" Since she'd perched precariously on the end of her desk, he moved the cup of water before she accidentally knocked it over.

"Taylor had an accident. The paramedics are there. I've got to go—Taylor's refusing to leave because she was watching Allie. I don't even know if my little girl's okay."

Oakley's voice was like calming music. "She's fine or the paramedics would have called you. I'll come with you. Don't even think of arguing. Since you don't live far, it'll be faster if we go on foot rather than trying to get the car out of the garage."

They walked quickly and arrived to find Taylor reclining on the gurney in obvious pain. "I misjudged the steps," she said. "I think I might have broken it."

Rachel winced. "You need to let them take you to the hospital. Where's Allie?"

"Here." Lisa stepped out of the studio. Allie's round face was bright red from the tears.

"We've all been taking turns holding her. She's adorable. She just wasn't used to all the new people."

"I'm so sorry she disturbed your class. Come here, sweetheart. It's okay."

Seeing her mother, Allie dove from Lisa's arms and into Rachel's. She buried her face in Rachel's shoulder.

"I called my daughter," Taylor said as the paramedics secured the safety straps. "She'll meet me at the hospital. I'll keep you posted as to babysitting tomorrow."

"Don't worry about Allie. You need to take care of yourself," Rachel said.

"I'll try," Taylor said with a wince.

The paramedics unlocked the wheels. "She's going to

need surgery. Most likely she won't be climbing any stairs for a while," one of them said.

"I'm fine," Taylor insisted, but her grimace revealed her lie.

"I'll come by tonight and visit," Rachel promised. The paramedics rolled her neighbor out to the ambulance, and Rachel carried Allie upstairs.

"At least she wasn't hurt worse," Rachel said. She put Allie in her high chair and gave her some Cheerios. "Taylor needs to heal, so I'm going to have to make other arrangements for Allie. The center doesn't have any child-care openings, and there's no elevator in this building. Most likely Taylor's going to need to stay on one floor for a long time. And even when she can climb the stairs, she can't take care of Allie. I can't ask that of her."

"Hey, it'll be okay." Oakley put his hands gently on her shoulders and she immediately felt far steadier. He had a magical touch, one that could both soothe or raise her temperature, depending on what the moment required. "Tell you what, bring her to work with you. We can create a nursery space where the visitor chairs are. It's not like we ever have anyone waiting. If needed, we can bring in one of those temporary dividers. You can also work from home as much as you'd like."

Working from home would mean she wouldn't see him. Since Dallas they already had a space the size of the Pacific Ocean between them. If he never saw her anywhere but online might he want to replace her with an in-office admin? "How about I spend two days in office and three days at home?" she proposed.

He lifted his hands, and she missed his touch. "Whatever you'd like. Do you trust me to have my concierge buy the things she'll need? Please let me do this for you.

Besides, they'll go to good use when we expand the office. This is proof my company needs its own on-site childcare facilities. I'll tell the relocation department to add it to the list."

"I trust you." She did, implicitly. "I'd probably be more effective if she's with me than if you and I are constantly having to video-call. Let me bring her into the office the next two days, and we can reassess from there."

"That works for me. Consider yourself off for the rest of the day."

"Actually, I brought my laptop," Rachel told him. "Allie's about to go down for her nap. If you're willing, we could both work here."

He nodded. "I'll walk back to the office and grab what I need. Did you eat lunch yet?" He noted the shake of her head. "I'll pick something up for both of us. See you soon."

With that, he left the apartment. Once he returned, she left Allie in his care and went to straighten and lock Taylor's apartment. When she came back, Oakley had Allie on his lap. She was patting his lips. "Dada da," she sang happily. Rachel's heart seized. The scene was too precious, the man she adored and her daughter clearly besotted with each other. This is what she wanted.

Rachel handed Oakley a sippy cup filled with formula, and he passed it to Allie. "Sadly, she has no idea what those words mean yet." She didn't want to hurt him, but she had to put things into perspective. She was already half in love with him and falling as fast as her daughter.

"Well, gives me all the feels anyway." Smiling, he gestured to the paper bag. "Eat. I brought sub sandwiches from the deli. I'm going to hold this little wiggler until you've gotten some food in you. Then you can put her down for her nap."

Allie was content to sit on Oakley's lap. Her daughter was a great judge of character, and Rachel wished she could bottle this moment. Still, she knew it was dangerous to think this way, to let herself imagine how she and Oakley could make the perfect family. If only she didn't work for him. If only his dad wasn't Clemons Fortune…

Life was a series of *if onlys*—of choices not made, paths not followed, of wishes that would never be fulfilled. Tomorrow might be a new day, but it wouldn't be the same as yesterday. Allie would take her first steps any day now, and from there she'd start running, and then driving, and then in the blink of an eye, Rachel would find herself dropping her daughter off at college and saying goodbye. She made a mental note to call her mother and tell her how much she loved her. After tossing her sandwich wrapper in the trashcan, she put her baby down for a nap and she and Oakley got to work.

By the time Allie woke, they'd finished their workload. They'd also found out from Taylor's daughter that she had a tibia/fibula ankle fracture. Taylor couldn't bear any weight for two weeks, and she'd need rehab after that. She'd either be on crutches or in a boot, which meant she wouldn't be available to babysit Allie for at least a month, perhaps more. Until the doctor cleared her to return home, she'd be staying with her daughter.

Oakley readied to leave. "Good thing we're putting in a temporary nursery. I'll see you in the office tomorrow morning, little one," He leaned and made a razzing sound that made Allie clap her hands. Turning back to Rachel, he gave her a warm smile. "And I'll see you, too, and have everything set up by the time you get there."

As her heart swelled, Rachel simply nodded and trailed him to the door. "You're too kind." He was Mr. Perfect, and she longed to tell him, to touch him...

He paused as if wanting to say something but shrugged it off. "See you in the morning."

Rachel locked the door behind him. She had to get these roller-coaster feelings under control. That proved easier said than done, especially when she saw firsthand the next morning how Oakley had transformed the office.

First, he had installed an intercom system. The exit door to the hall would remain locked at all times, and visitors who arrived would push a button. Once Rachel saw who was at the door, she could buzz them inside. This way Allie would not be disturbed and random people could not simply walk in. There was a doorman downstairs, but it was a busy office building. Next, Oakley had a carpenter set up a temporary barrier that divided Rachel's office into two parts. The part closest to the kitchen and bathroom became a small nursery fitted with a crib where Allie could nap, and a changing table. He'd installed a camera so Rachel could see Allie, and he'd had the entire office babyproofed. A high chair was crammed into the small kitchen, and in the main area, Allie's playpen was near Rachel's desk. There was also a new bookcase covered in toys.

Rachel found the biggest distraction was that Oakley kept coming out of his office to play with Allie. He adored her daughter. He loved holding her, and had even done so during a video call with Clark. Since the door was open, Rachel had heard everyone laughing.

Now, as Oakley came into the doorway, he smiled at Rachel and Allie, who was crawling across the cleaned carpet. "Sorry, tonight will be a late one," he said. "I've got dinner set to be delivered around six."

"It's okay." She'd known about the late meeting for several weeks, long before Taylor's accident. A group of investors had approached Oakley about doing a rodeo showcase in Japan. When the call connected at 7:00 p.m. Texas time, it would be 9:00 a.m. the next day in Tokyo. It was an incredible avenue to broaden Oakley's market share.

"It's an exciting opportunity," Oakley confessed as he ate his pasta. "My mom always wanted to go to Japan, so it's almost like fulfilling a dream if I do."

"You've done well for yourself."

"I try. As long as Mom wouldn't chide me about being a workaholic or refusing to relax. In fact, the last time I relaxed was in Dallas, with you."

Rachel felt her cheeks heat. She remembered Dallas as if it had been yesterday. "Your mom would be very proud of you."

"I hope so. The way I was brought up is one of the reasons for my drive and nonstop work habits," he admitted. "I always worry about bringing my dad up when I'm with you, but I have to for you to fully understand why I'm the way I am. My dad's adoptive family might be rich, but they believe you make it on your own. They're not giving Clemons any money until they pass, if then. Trouble is that my dad is not good at business. He had all these silly get rich schemes, and not one ever took off, and raising six kids was expensive. He just got by financially when he and my mom got married, and it didn't get better, until he started suing everyone in sight and made his first real fortune. In the first lawsuits he had some justification. In yours, he didn't."

"No, he didn't." Rachel ate some of the delicious pasta con broccoli.

"After my mom passed, and as he got worse with his absurd litigations, I'll admit to being embarrassed by my dad's actions. I wanted to build my business and fortune differently from how he made his. In order to put my business in the black, I became a workaholic. I was determined to prove that, unlike my dad's failures, it could be done."

She resisted the urge to reassure him by touching his hand. "Your efforts paid off. You're about to embark on your biggest enterprise to date. Japan sounds fantastic. I've always wanted to go there."

"Well, if I get this, I'll be sure you get that chance. You've been my right hand, and I wouldn't be here without you."

He locked eyes with her and Rachel caught her breath. She ducked her head, breaking the contact first. She could not dare to dream.

"I better go freshen up and study my notes again," he said.

"Good idea." She rose and busied herself with cleaning the dishes, for escaping to the kitchen allowed her to get her heartbeat under control.

When it was time for the call, he closed the door to his office. He was still online an hour later when Rachel put Allie to bed. She'd hate waking her to move her into her car seat for the drive home, but it couldn't be helped. Allie, though, was pretty good about going right back to sleep.

Around eight-thirty, Oakley opened the door. "How'd it go?" Rachel asked as she stifled a yawn. She'd finished most of her work thirty minutes ago.

"It went great. I need you to type up the notes I took and send them over to Dallas so they can review first thing and start drafting our proposal. Then let's go home." Even though she knew he meant going to their respective residences, she liked how when he said "home," it sent a quiver through her.

"Give me a few minutes and I'll be done."

"Thanks." He went to check on Allie. He returned carrying two bottles of water. "Thought you might like some hydration." He set a bottle on the corner of her desk and went inside his office.

She'd gotten used to reading his handwriting, and while she typed up his notes, she received several emails she'd been copied on. He'd sent his executives a list of urgent action items, and also scheduled follow-up meetings with his Dallas staff. She sent him his notes for review, and that email pinged into her inbox as well once distributed.

Ready to leave, she went to his office doorway and found him silhouetted in the dark. He stared out the window at the night sky and street below. He turned. "Sorry. I was just thinking. Mostly I was processing the implications of what my team and I discussed tonight. I'm trying to anticipate any roadblocks. If we get this, we might need to hire additional staff and move the office early."

"That's fantastic, isn't it?" She could feel the waves of excitement radiating from him.

"It is." He grinned as he crossed the semi-lit space. "I couldn't have done it without your help. We make such a great team, you and I. The best. I'm so lucky to have you."

All she'd done was type up notes, but the closer he came, the more of an electric undercurrent pulsed between them. His two computer screens created a blue-green glow, and a small green banker's desk lamp created a pathway of illumination that seemed to lead Oakley to Rachel. "Rachel, I..."

"Oakley..."

Their use of each other's names heightened whatever had been growing between them. "I'm not supposed to be feeling this way," he said huskily. "But I can't help it. Not touching you, especially after what happened in Dallas, not being with you is *torture*."

"I agree. I've hated this," she whispered, for kissing him again was as essential as taking her next breath. She reached to cup his cheek and bring his face lower. When their lips touched, the fireworks began.

Or maybe it was stars she saw. She certainly felt the chemistry flaring between them. It carried the kiss to the next level, as if a rocket raced toward the stratosphere. She wanted Oakley. She wanted to risk, to tumble into the oblivion and worry about tomorrow, well, tomorrow.

"Touch me," she urged, and soon his hands were everywhere. He undid the buttons of her dress shirt. He fingered the lace strap of her black bra.

His breath hissed on the intake. "Beautiful. A sexy little surprise."

"I bought it in Dallas. I wore it under the red dress."

His caressing fingers hardened her nipples to points. "Had I known this was underneath we might not have made it to the cocktail party."

"Good thing you didn't then." Her teasing was lost to the tantalizing movement of his fingertips.

"But I do now." The straps went around her biceps, and then the pretty bra was no more, banished to the floor. She felt a hint of nerves as he traced her skin. After nursing for a few months, her breasts hadn't regained their pre-pregnancy smaller size or perkiness, but when he cupped them in his hand, he declared them perfect, and then she was in his arms and he gently placed her on the couch and followed her down.

As his mouth found her neck and moved lower, Rachel realized that the intense sensations came from the rare and elemental connection she and Oakley shared. This was more than meeting physical needs. This joining was transformative and earth-shattering. His tongue swirled over her nipples until her hands clutched his back and tremors shook her body.

And that was simply the appetizer as his mouth moved lower, until he stopped by the waistband of her skirt. As that, too, was an unneeded piece of clothing, instead of simply lifting it, he slid it down. Oakley found her core and licked into her heat. Her limbs became jelly. She could do nothing but let him take over. He brushed aside her hands when she reached for him. He gave and gave, taking her to heights she didn't realize could be reached. He did more than reset her body postbirth. He helped her chart a fresh course. She felt like a phoenix rising from the ashes of her past. When he touched her, he rewrote her code, changing her and making her renewed. She'd lost count of the orgasms, or the ways his fingers could be so gentle yet so precise as they roamed her body creating unique erogenous zones, both inside and out.

He was in no hurry to end the foreplay, and the more she came, the more she discovered she was the one who was impatient. "You're wearing too many clothes," she complained.

"Let me worship you." He gently lifted one of her hands above her head and stretched out her arm. "I've wanted to do this since Dallas. Heck, probably since the first day we met. Please."

So she let him continue, for who could resist that pleasurable plea? He'd made the night about her pleasure, not his. She was floating down from another orgasm when he finally gave her what she wanted by shedding his shirt. She placed both hands on his chest, the ensuing heat coursing through her palms. She marveled at the smooth texture of hard, chiseled muscle. He had a body sculpted by the gods. The sensation flowing through her was divine mystery, that promise of bliss and something still undefined that had to be experienced.

"Are you sure?" he asked her.

She nodded. It took her a moment to find her voice. "Yes. I'm sure."

In one of those miracles of time, he was naked and protected before she could think to ask him, and his powerful arms surrounded her as he poised at her entrance. He hovered until their gazes locked, and then he was inside her, and Rachel's head moved to rest against the arm of the couch as another round of sensations began. She had no idea where she ended and he began, but the only thing that truly mattered was how he made her feel.

Incredible. Blissful. Joyous. Changed. Whole. Perfect. Beautiful. Orgasmic.

The dictionary didn't contain enough words. Their coupling was everything and more, a transcendence of emotion and physicality. This was lovemaking.

Not what she'd experienced before. That had been a prelude, a false flag. Going through the motions. Even in Dallas, there had been some lingering doubts.

This was true lovemaking. *This.* What was happening, right here. Right now.

With Oakley. The difference between sex and lovemaking was as clear as the orgasm overtaking her, causing her legs to shake. Her hands attempted to find purchase on the leather.

He brought her to the place where thoughts disappeared and pleasure reigned supreme, and when she exploded, it felt as if she was being remade, her body yielding like soft clay beneath his every touch.

He held her gently afterward. Planted kisses on her face and lips. Pressed his forehead to hers. "Incredible. Everything I dreamed this time would be."

In that languid state of fluid aftermath, she could only nod at the wonderment as he shifted to hold her close, his arms tight around her. She'd never felt so secure.

This was yet another moment that she wished she could capture, though she had no doubt she'd remember it forever. Her heart felt split open, and she bit her lip to keep from blurting out the three words that would change everything. But that revelation—*that this had been so much more than sex for her*—had to remain her secret.

She had no idea of Oakley's feelings. Mitch had taught her that men were different, that they could compartmentalize. Things that meant everything to a woman could mean nothing to a man.

Allie's cry coming through the camera feed in the other room was a welcome distraction, and her skin cooled as Oakley released her. She threw on her clothes. By the time she returned with a freshly diapered Allie in her arms, Oakley was dressed and hard to read. "You good?" he asked.

Rachel wasn't sure to whom he referred, her or Allie. "We're good. I'm going to get her home."

"Okay. I'll walk you to your car. It's next to mine."

Now what? Rachel thought. They'd given into their lust again, and awkwardness descended as they closed the office. This feeling of despair, of facing the unknown and the morning after, was what she'd wanted to avoid, why they'd tried to go back to what they were after that first time in Dallas. They'd have to discuss this. Could they go back to being professional? Try again?

She had a feeling that ship had sailed. But she had no idea where she stood. What came next? What did he want from her? It's not like he'd asked for a relationship, even if he'd suggested she deserved one. He hadn't offered to file human resources paperwork. They went out into the brightly lit parking garage, which Rachel thought was akin to the lights coming on in a bar after closing time. The overhead lighting exposed everything and brought home instant regret. She secured Allie's car seat and climbed into her car.

"I'll follow you out." He gave her a kiss on the lips that contained none of the passion of earlier. "Text me when you're home safe."

"I will. And don't forget I won't be in tomorrow. I'm working from home." It was one of her scheduled days.

"Thanks for reminding me. I'll miss seeing you." But his smile didn't reach his eyes, leaving her with doubts. "Remember, text me."

He shut the car door and moved aside so she could back out. Rachel texted him a short time later, letting him know she'd put Allie into her crib and ensured she was back asleep.

He "liked" her message, but that was it.

Rachel stared at the phone screen as if willing it to do something. Nothing else was forthcoming, nor had any text or voicemail arrived by the time she went to bed. While she had the phone set to Do Not Disturb, she'd given permissions to Oakley's number so that his messages and calls always came through.

Yet nothing did, and the silence was worse than a ticking clock or buzzing fly. Worry built and mixed with regret, and as the combination brewed, Rachel gnawed her lower lip. She'd slept with her boss. She'd made love to Oakley. Again.

Her boss and Oakley might be the same person, but they were worlds apart in mission and personality. Worse, she was in love with both. This crash came fast, especially as she had no one to blame but herself.

Just what had she done?

Chapter Thirteen

Oakley was not the type who kicked himself, but the next day at the office, as he stared at Rachel's empty desk, that's what he did, over and over. How could he have let things go so far? The first time they'd been dancing and living in the moment. She'd been in a sexy dress. They'd gotten carried away. He had none of those excuses for last night. While every step of the way had been mutual, confirmed by asking her consent, he'd let his desires overrule his common sense. He had to be strictly professional from now on. He was treading on dangerous ground.

He was already way too deep. He'd built a nursery in the office, for goodness' sake! He picked up one of Allie's toys and set it back in the playpen.

Oakley sat at his desk and wiggled in his chair to get comfortable, which was hard to do as he kept staring at the couch where he'd had the best sex of his life. It had been transcendent, everything he'd hoped for. He'd dreamed of finding such a woman, and she'd been right in front of him all along. But doubts remained, planted by his brother, who'd warned him to avoid doing the very thing Oakley had done. And what did he do next? He felt as awkward as a gangly teen on his first date who had no clue how to lean in and kiss the girl. What would Rachel be thinking? Did she have regrets? Should he have stopped them from falling into bed like he'd promised her in Dallas?

When Rachel had started working from home, they'd established a ritual of having coffee every morning. He logged onto his computer and brought up the video conferencing program and clicked their chat link. He found her in the virtual space, but her microphone was off, and so was her video feed. He had both of his on. She'd see him and unmute soon.

The ceramic mug emblazoned with his company logo was warm in his hand but did little to calm the chill traveling through him. Let everything be normal, he prayed. Then the screen flickered, and she came into focus. "Good morning," he said. "How'd you sleep?"

"Fine. You?"

"Like a log." They were both lying, and they knew it.

"That's great. I heard back from Augustus in response to the email I sent two days ago..."

So this is how she wanted to handle things, by *ignoring* them. Fine—he could do that. But he found his mind wandering as their meeting progressed. His computer monitor did nothing to keep him from remembering the softness of her skin, or the way her lips had felt under his, or the way she'd tasted on his tongue. Twice he had to ask her to repeat herself before he managed to buckle down and concentrate.

When she put Allie on her lap, his mind lost focus again, especially when the baby saw him and began babbling *dada dada*. He'd crossed a line by letting himself care for both of them. He'd been what she'd said she didn't want: unethical and unprofessional. When she lifted Allie's hand and waved it at him, a tremor of regret ran through him.

"We should probably talk about last night," he said.

Whatever bright light had been in her eyes dimmed. “Okay,” she said.

“We’ve…well… I…” He faltered. “We clearly have a chemistry between us,” he told her. “But…”

“Let me put Allie in her playpen.” Her chair remained empty on the monitor until she returned and her face came into view. “Okay,” Rachel said, her expression now unreadable. When she didn’t say anything else, it was clear she was going to make him start. Whatever he said, it would have huge implications. He felt damned if he did, damned if he didn’t.

“I can’t deny I’m attracted to you,” he began, already sensing he was on shaky ground, especially as they both knew another *but* was coming. Perhaps he should have asked her thoughts first. Was she in love with him? Could she be? Did they want to try to date and have a relationship? Should he bring that up?

“We work together…” He faltered again. He’d just made the error of starting the conversation from the position of her boss, and suddenly he was like a runaway train, unable to stop. “Despite an obvious attraction and a mind-blowing night, we work together.”

“Yes, I know.” Her tone was clipped and tight, her face a cold mask. For a man who had built a thriving business, he was blowing this.

“I promise to be strictly professional from now on. I’d also understand if you choose to quit. If you do, I’ll pay your salary until you find an equal or better job. I’ll also give you a glowing reference.”

“Really? I see. That’s generous. How kind of you.”

Oakley could see he’d stunned her and not in a good way. She glanced away from the video. He willed her to look at him, but she didn't. He didn't want her to quit—he wanted her to choose him.

He could tell he'd blown this. But before he could ask about her true feelings, she swiveled back to the camera but didn't raise her eyes to look at him. "Is there anything else? I think I hear Allie."

There were tons of things he wanted to say. He'd messed up. But he worried if they kept talking, he might ruin things even more. He needed to retrench and think. Figure out what to say. "We can talk later. Go get her. She's your priority." Since the video ended as she exited the call, he wasn't certain if she'd heard him.

He yanked a hand through his hair before banging his fist against the table. Several pens rattled inside the holder. He exhaled a curse word. Why had he told her she could quit? He rubbed his fingers against his temples. Somehow he had to salvage things. But for the first time, he had no idea how.

Hours later, as night fell, Rachel lifted Allie from her playpen. She clutched her daughter tightly. "You're the one great thing in my life," she whispered before putting Allie into her crib. She sat on the edge of her bed as her daughter fell asleep. "What am I going to do now?" she asked the universe. She'd had the worst day ever. She'd say she'd done her job like a robot, except for the tears that had threatened over and over. She'd been grateful she'd been able to communicate with Oakley via email and nothing else. Seeing him would break her heart more. She couldn't keep doing this. Not when it was clear he didn't return her feelings. She reached for her phone and texted Jenny and told her she wanted to talk. Within two seconds, Jenny called her.

"You never contact me this late with something so cryptic unless something's wrong. What happened?"

Rachel nibbled her lip and couldn't bring herself to admit that she'd botched things up by sleeping with her boss.

"Oh, honey." Jenny's sympathy and understanding radiated across the distance. "Your silence says it all. It's bad, isn't it? It's only seven. I'm on my way."

Jenny arrived twenty minutes later with two pints of ice cream from Emerald Ridge's local creamery. She passed a plastic spoon and the Rocky Road flavor to Rachel. "Unless you want vanilla bean?"

"No." Rachel removed the lid, set it on the coffee table and dug her spoon inside the chocolate, marshmallow and nut-flavored ice cream. She tucked her legs underneath her as she ate a few bites. "You know Rocky Road is my favorite."

"Which is why I got it for you. What's going on, Rachel? Talk to me."

"Last night I had sex with Oakley. In his office, on the couch." The words poured forth, including the rest of what had happened, and ending with his severance offer. "Jenny, I ruined everything."

"I'm sure that's not true," her friend soothed.

"It is." She swallowed a lump in her throat. "I'm falling in love with him, but he has no feelings for me." As the reality set in, she started crying.

"Are you sure? Have you asked him?" Jenny put the lid back on her ice cream. She handed Rachel a napkin, which she used to dab her eyes.

"I can't. It would be too painful if he says no. A girl has to have her pride."

Jenny tried to be the voice of reason. "You can quit, Rachel. I'll help you find another job. In fact, go to the office tomorrow and collect your things. I'll watch Allie for you while you give your notice."

"I loved this job." The tears flowed again. "Everyone was so nice."

"I'll find you one better," Jenny vowed. She reached for both ice cream pints and put them in the freezer. "It's going to be okay, Rachel. I promise. Bring Allie to the house first thing. I'll work from home tomorrow."

"Thank you. You're a good friend." Rachel threw herself into the other woman's arms. "I messed up. Maybe ruined your business."

"No, you didn't, and I'm always your friend first, Rachel. And whatever you decide, I'm on your side, okay? Oakley's a great guy. Find out how he feels. Talk to him."

"Why do I feel like I'm about to lose everything again?" Rachel moaned.

"You won't. But at least you will know where you stand. Maybe he'll declare his undying love, and you'll ride off into the sunset together."

Rachel's heart leaped at the thought, but she tamped the overwhelming emotions down. She was an adult. A mother. She could do hard things and had proven that over and over again. This would be yet another example. Princes didn't fall in love with girls like her. They simply fell into bed.

The next morning, Rachel was already at her desk when Oakley arrived. "Good morning," he said as he came through the door.

"Good morning," she replied, and when she shifted, he noticed the small cardboard box she'd set under her desk. She was leaving.

As panic clawed him, his gaze scanned her face and

tried to read the expression she'd schooled into neutral. She rose to her feet, revealing she'd worn far more casual clothes than she usually did. She'd made a decision. She was quitting, and there was nothing he could do to stop her.

"I've placed your agenda on your desk, filed the papers that needed filing and set things up for the day."

"Thank you. Rachel, are you sure you want this?" His arms folded over his chest and immediately recognizing the defensive gesture, he loosened his limbs. "I know I need to apologize for yesterday morning, and that if I seemed too abrupt or..."

"It's fine," she said hurriedly, her eagerness to leave making him freeze as she reached to retrieve the box. "It's fine, Oakley. Let's be honest. It needed to be said. We can't keep going on like this, so I've decided to accept your severance offer. Jenny and I discussed it last night. In fact, she's watching Allie for me today while I collect my things. She'll find me a new position."

"I see." He didn't move, although he wanted to gather her in his arms and convince her to stay. He felt the corner of his cheek twitch as he tried to keep the emotions in check. Part of him wanted to argue, another part ached to beg for forgiveness and ask her to stay. He felt torn in two, as if someone had taken dull scissors to his heart and chopped with abandon, caring little for how much it hurt. She was so beautiful. He wanted her to be his completely, in all aspects.

"At least now, if we're not working together, we won't have to worry about avoiding our physical attraction," he said.

As her face whitened, he realized he'd said the wrong thing again. He winced. In business, he was Mr. Cool and Collected. He made deals with a flick of his wrist. But he couldn't get the correct words out with Rachel to save his life. She picked up the box, which he saw was already loaded, the photo of Allie on the top. His heart shattered.

"Oakley, I'm grateful you gave me this opportunity. I won't regret what we shared. But we can't continue, and you and I know that. As you said once, I'm worth more."

He blanched as he realized she thought he was only interested in her physically. "Rachel, I…"

She already had her hand on the door. Oakley reached for her arm but let his fall. He didn't have the right to touch her. She'd made up her mind. How many times had his ex-wife done this, and he'd tried to make things work? He couldn't fix this. He had to let Rachel go. He might love her—damn right he did. Why did that realization come too late? But loving someone meant respecting their decisions. Oakley knew he'd been selfish in the past. He'd been so determined to fix his marriage that he'd kept convincing his ex to stay even though she'd wanted to leave. While it didn't excuse her cheating, he'd been wrong to pressure her. He'd wanted the idea of marriage so greatly that he'd been trying to make things work even when he knew they weren't.

He couldn't fall back into the same old patterns. He'd chased Rachel once. He'd violated their agreement by making love to her. And saying he loved her now would come across as a manipulation. He wouldn't be that man ever again. He couldn't be.

She had the door to the hall open. "I'm sorry things didn't work out," he said hoarsely. "I'll get in touch with Jenny and work out the details."

She gave a nod and dipped her head. "It's been nice knowing you."

Before he could react, the door had already closed.

Chapter Fourteen

Rachel balanced the cardboard box as she walked home. She entered the apartment, which was silent since Allie was at Jenny's. She set her things on the kitchen table. How easily one's work life fit into a small box. She lifted the portrait and set it on the counter. While it was usually wonderful to have the place to herself, today was not one of those times. She couldn't sit here or she'd wallow. It was a lovely day, so she'd go to Jenny's, pick up Allie and take her daughter to the park.

She should probably go to the bakery first and grab something as a thank-you for Jenny. Her bestie had brought wine and ice cream last night. The least Rachel could do was bring doughnuts. She grabbed her house key and phone and headed downstairs. Once out of her apartment building door, she rounded the corner to Emerald Ridge Boulevard and she bumped into a rock-solid object.

"You!" she said as she recoiled in horror. "Don't you dare think of suing me for walking into you when you were the one not paying attention!"

It was then she noticed the tears in Clemons Fortune's eyes. "Are you okay?" she asked as she peered at him. "I didn't hurt you." There was a camera on the corner that would prove it.

"For once, it's not you." He reached into his pocket and shoved a flyer into her hand. "Have you seen my cat?"

Rachel almost dropped the flyer she was so surprised, first by his anguish and now by his speaking to her in a tone that was more pleading than accusatory.

"No. I told you I didn't let your cat out. I have no idea where it is."

His signature suit coat was missing, and his shirt and his linen pants were rumpled. "I know… I'm sorry about that. I was angry. You were there and I lashed out. Oakley told me I shouldn't be rude. Sometimes I can't help myself. My wife would be ashamed."

She didn't want to say, "It's okay," for it wasn't. But she was not a vindictive person. "I can see you miss her very much."

"I do." The tears grew, and he reached into his pants pocket for a handkerchief. He dabbed his eyes. "You think you'll have a lifetime together and then it's gone."

"We'll find your cat. But surely it's not here, in the central business district?"

"I don't know. Because of the reward on the flyers, we've had so many leads. I'm tracking down every tip that I get. I even brought in a woman who uses dogs to track Mewington's scent, but while we pinpointed an area, we couldn't find him when we searched. I'm starting to doubt anyone's seen him."

"Would you like me to help you look?" she offered.

He blinked at her with eyes wide in surprise. "Why would you help me? I've been awful to you. I accused you of stealing him."

Rachel didn't have an answer to that. Her innate sense of empathy had made her mouth speak before her brain had the opportunity to tell her mouth to shut up.

"I'd like the help…and appreciate the company," he continued. "And again, I'm sorry. I've been so wrong about you. My son trusts you, and if Oakley hired you as his admin, I should trust you, too."

It hurt too much to tell him she was no longer his son's admin. She was there to find a cat, that was all. "If I say I'm helping, then I help," Rachel said as they went down the alley and began searching under some commercial trash receptacles.

After about fifteen minutes of searching the alley, with her checking one side and Clemons peering around the other, they still hadn't found Mewington. They'd even looked down several of the cross streets. They walked back toward Emerald Ridge Boulevard. "I'm stopping at the bakery café for doughnuts," she said. "May I buy you a cup of coffee?"

"I'd like that," Clemons responded, as he held open the door for her. "We're not far from your office. Should we text Oakley to see what he wants?"

"If you'd like. I'm happy to get him something, but you need to know that I turned in my notice. Yesterday was my last day."

Even saying the words hurt, and Clemons ushered her to a small table. "After everything, this is on me. What would you like?"

"No, I said I'd treat." Using the app on her phone and the QR code on the table, Rachel placed their order.

"Will you tell me what happened?" Clemons asked gruffly. "He was so happy with you. I know I was awful to you, but like I said, I was out of line. Me and my big mouth—I didn't mean it. Oakley was right to yell at me."

"You *were* awful," she agreed. After today, unless she

spilled coffee on him, hopefully this branch of the Fortune family was out of her life for good.

"I overreacted. I just saw that Oakley was clearly in love with you and that rattled me. His ex-wife did a number on his head. She hurt him. And then there was his previous admin who tried to trap him by being overtly sexual. I projected my fears onto you. My son is old enough to handle himself."

His dad thought Oakley loved her? She couldn't believe that. But before she could tell Clemons he was wrong, her name was called. She went to the counter and returned with the doughnuts and coffees.

"You're a decent person, Rachel. A good mom, like my Randa was. I can see why Oakley cares for you. I know I'm an old curmudgeon. I'm set in my ways, and half the time I'm embarrassing my kids. I'm trying to change…" Clemons scrubbed a hand over his face, his voice cracking slightly. "They say it's time to get over the sadness and the heartbreak, but none of them have been married for thirty-five years like Randa and I were. It's not been the same since I lost her. There's a giant hole where my heart used to be."

He chewed some of the glazed doughnut. "It's like the universe is angry with me. Now my precious Mewington is gone. The house feels too empty. You have Allie, but I have nothing. Not even my kids if I don't change my ways. But it's hard for an old fool like me."

"I do have Allie, and I have the example of my parents' loving marriage. You and your wife set that for your children. They just want you happy."

"You made Oakley happy," Clemons said. He opened the lid of his coffee, looked at it unhappily and put the lid back on.

"Yes, but we're not meant to be." How she wished that were different!

"How do you know?"

Rachel sipped her coffee. No way was she wading into a conversation with Oakley's father about how his son simply wanted to sleep with her and nothing more.

Clemons wiped his fingers on a paper napkin. "If it's because I called you a gold digger, you're not, and I'm truly sorry I said that. It was terrible and untrue. You and Oakley care for each other, and it's clear your heart is broken. I can sense these things."

"Fine. He and I don't have the same goals for a relationship. He also feels that he wouldn't be good for me. Told me that I deserve more than what he can give."

Clemons gave a frustrated exhale. "That son of mine often can't see what's right in front of him. You need to be more like me. Tell him what you want. Be straightforward. That's how you get the results you deserve. Stop holding back your feelings. Don't wait. Time is short."

"Perhaps, but that's true only to a degree. What do *you* want, Clemons? What would make you happy?"

He scowled. "Well, it's not to have you turn this around on me. This is about you getting your man."

"Sorry." But she couldn't help but smile, and soon he did, too.

"You got gumption, Rachel. I'm glad we had this little chat. Now, as much as I thank you for this coffee, you need to go because I have to head over to the counter and tell them they didn't fill my cup correctly."

"You're right." She had no desire to see that. "I'm going to go home, figure things out and chat with Oakley." Thankfully she hadn't texted Jenny yet about picking Allie up early. "Good luck finding your cat."

"Thank you." As Clemons headed toward the counter, she disposed of the trash and headed back to her apartment, bag of doughnuts in one hand and her to-go cup in the other. Could she and Oakley have a chance? She loved him. If Clemons—her former enemy—thought her worthy, maybe she should try. She turned the corner and frowned. Someone was sitting in her doorway. Her sense of caution kicking in, adrenaline pumped as she edged to the outside of the sidewalk. "Oakley?" Relief was quickly replaced with worry. "What are you doing here? Has something happened? How long have you been sitting there?"

He uncoiled to his full height. "Twenty, thirty minutes? I lost track."

"Why didn't you text me if you needed something?"

"Because what I need is you, Rachel. Not just physically, but in every aspect. Mentally. Emotionally. All of it. I'm madly in love with you." He swallowed hard. "I want you, Rachel, all of you, including Allie. You walked into my office that first day, and it was like I'd known you my whole life. I've never been this comfortable with anyone the way I am with you. You make me complete."

"Oh." Rachel found herself at a loss for words and she clutched the bakery bag tighter.

"The other day I messed up. I didn't want to tell you my true feelings because I was your boss. I thought, if I did, I would be manipulating you or being selfish, like my ex said I could be. I know I can be too focused on work, but, Rachel, I want you."

Rachel searched his face and found him sincere. She could hardly believe it, but Oakley meant what he said so earnestly.

"I haven't expressed it well, but the truth is I care for

you a great deal. I don't want this to be one-sided. I want an equal partnership. Me and you. In life. In love. In business, if we want. But mostly, in marriage. That's where I'm going, Rachel. I want you forever. The rest will work itself out as long as we love each other. And I think you love me. I hope you love me."

"I do. I love you, too," she said, tears of joy beginning to run down her face. "You're everything I could have wanted. I was actually about to come find you and tell you that. I realized our conversation wasn't finished. That the Oakley I love would never just want me for sex. I should have heard you out and not walked away."

"I want you, Rachel, darling. Everything. All of it. The good times and bad, the better or worse, and all the rest. I wish we hadn't wasted even a minute."

"I agree." She sniffed. "From here on, we have to say what we think. Be straight shooters like your dad and speak our minds to each other."

"Why are you are quoting my dad?"

"Well, amazingly enough, we just had doughnuts." As Oakley drew her into his arms, she explained.

"I don't often thank my dad for things, but for this, I'll forever be grateful." Oakley held her tightly. "He brought you back to me."

"Well, don't get too excited. He was about to go complain about the coffee when I left," Rachel teased. "Now, enough about your dad. Did I tell you that Jenny is watching Allie?"

"Is she?" Oakley's fingers pushed Rachel's hair behind her ears. "That sounds promising."

"Yes, especially because I don't have to pick her up until later." Stepping partially out of Oakley's grasp, Rachel unlocked the door to her building. "Shall we go upstairs?"

"I love you," he said as he swept her into his arms and carried her up the stairs, pastry bag and all. "And just so you know, as soon as you're ready, you're moving in with me. You and Allie. Because I want forever. Is that direct enough?"

Her heart filled. "Very direct."

"Good. Because I meant it when I said I love you. And I'm going to show you, starting right now and for every minute for the rest of our lives."

And as he kissed her, Rachel realized that maybe, after all, dreams really did come true.

* * * * *